Xeyata

Xeyata

Up on the Mountain

A Fiction
About a young boy whose
Responsibility
Is to perform the
Turn of the Century Ceremony

Violet H. Catches

Xeyata Up On The Mountain

A young boy's duty to make a millennium ritual happen for his tribal nation ... the Lakxota. (Lakota)

Order this book online at www.trafford.com
or email orders@trafford.com

Most Trafford titles are also available at major online book retailers.

Printed in the United States of America.

ISBN: 978-1-4269-6112-0 (sc)
ISBN: 978-1-4269-6795-5 (hc)
ISBN: 978-1-4269-6111-3 (e)

Library of Congress Control Number: 2011907478

Trafford rev. 06/25/2011

 www.trafford.com

North America & International
toll-free: 1 888 232 4444 (USA & Canada)
phone: 250 383 6864 ♦ fax: 812 355 4082

Dedication

To *Txunkashila*, Creator, to the ancestors, to all the people who live today, to all those who are yet to come, to *kxatiye topa*, the four winds, to the sky above and beyond, to the core of the earth, to the things that move at night.

To my son Lester, whose accident brought this story about, to those who taught me at home to live this life, Unci Wasu, Uncila Sarah Holy, to Lala Robert Blue Hair, Lekshi Tokxala Martin Holy, Mama Mabel Mexican, Até Vincent Catches. To Lekshi Percy and Txuwin Delphine High Hawk; to Daniel and Bessie Dull Knife, who were like parents to me; and to Barb and Del Marie and all those whose influence and stories I retell in this book.

To those who encouraged me to stay in college at Native American Educational Studies (NAES) College in Chicago, who helped me find my true identity and form a new identity in this bicultural world that we live in. To those at the University of Colorado at Boulder, who helped me understand how my own language works and how to develop our own writing system or alphabet.

To the Northern Cheyenne people who are our relatives.

To my children, Merril, Jolene, Lawton, Doreen, Lester Jr., Candace, Sarah, and Edwin. To my adopted daughters, Florence and Katrina, and all my grandchildren including Jacob and Janell. To my nieces and nephews everywhere.

To my brothers and sisters, Veda, Marvin, Esterlita, and Carlos. And to my adopted sisters, Matilda and Ruth.

And all my relatives.

"Let us put our minds together to see what we can do for our children."
—Sitting Bull

Author's note

The past is not gone; the past is still with us in stories, song, and dance, in rituals and ceremony. It is our responsibility as grandparents to pass on the past, send it into the future to the next seven generations. The seventh generation is not an easy concept to understand. However, we in this generation need to pass on what we can and leave behind what needs to be left. What is to be left behind are the physical aspects of a life completed in this world. What can to be taken to the future is the teachings that flow from that physical life left behind.

That is the thought behind this story, because the Turn of the Century ceremony and its song are no longer talked about. The people who taught me were loving and kind people. My uncle Percy was a powwow singer. In our travels to powwows or back to the reservation, he would sing a song and tell us about the song. He sang the Turn of the Century song several times, but in general, people do not think about this song as being one of the important rituals of our nation.

He told us that when new grass appears each spring, people celebrate the arrival of a new year and a new beginning. It is the end of *waniyetu*, winter, and the end of a year. There is a song for every hundred years, he said, and then there is the millennium song and event, which is also connected to the stars, which he said he did not understand, as he was a boy when he was told.

My first language was Lakxota; my way of thinking was established in that language. The second language I heard was Latin, in our Catholic Church. I do not speak Latin. I understand and can respond to the prayers and sing songs in Latin. We can say that I was born into the

Lakxota and Latin languages. My third language was English, which we learned to speak in school.

I was born at home in Bridger, during a blizzard at night. It was at a time when a wake was being held for a woman who died that day. I was born Violet Helena Catches to Vincent and Mabel Holy-Catches, who were legally married at that time but physically apart.

As I grew, I spent my days following my grandmother around. She often talked to herself, telling stories of long ago. *"Ehani cha …"* is how her stories start, and they end, *"Ho, hechetu."* Sometimes, telling these stories, she would cry, and today sometimes I cry when I retell some of her stories. My formative first ten years were spent with Uncila Sarah. We did many things, like washing clothes in the river, going in a team and wagon to get drinking water, picking medicine for her brother who was a medicine man. Sometimes we went to visit relatives in the team and wagon to Red Scaffold and Cherry Creek and then back to Bridger.

When she passed on, I went to live with Uncle Percy and Aunt Delphine, then to the Dull Knifes, then I was on my own. Wherever I went to live, we used the Lakxota language to communicate. Songs and stories were told on the pow wow trail. That is how I learned of the "crazy woman" who lived in that cave now called Hell's Half Acre in Wyoming. Late one summer night, as we were on our way to Ethete, Wyoming, we stopped there, and Daniel told us the story about her. There are many more stories to tell. We need to find the time to collaborate as Lakxota women and men to pass on the stories we know. We cannot leave with the stories, so let's tell them. Ho, hechetu!

CONTENTS

Chapter 1
Birth of Kikto

Ehani cha, long ago, high in the mountains a people camped for the winter, as they did year after year, for an unknown number of years, perhaps centuries. There in a teepee lived Watxoye (Makes Blue) and his wife, Khugyuhamaniwin, which means Century Keeper Woman. Their daughter, Wichaxpi or Star, lived with her husband in the next teepee. A newborn child lay next to her. It was early spring, still chilly enough to keep the fire burning through the night. It was good that the stones in the firepit stayed hot throughout the night.

The newborn boy was a special child, born as predicted, a moon before he was expected. This boy was destined to learn the songs and rituals for the Turn of the Century ceremony. The family, through oral traditions, carried the story and the songs, along with sacred objects that he would need to pass on to future generations. The child's name, Kiktopawingxa, came from the female side of the family. There was a story connected to his name. For centuries, a story was passed down his mother's bloodline from generation to generation. Now it was time to enact this sacred ritual.

In her youth, Khugyuhamaniwin's *unci* or grandmother told her the story and said that in her lifetime, a sacred event would take place—perhaps unci would be here, perhaps not; even so, it would take place as predicted. Later, her ailing grandmother told her the story for the last time. This last telling included a passing of objects to her. Two winter counts, four gourds, and the words to the songs. Kiktopawingxa must grow up to do this sacred rite. This event would complete a cycle of life for many generations to help them live in harmony with all life. Khugyuhamaniwin thought about the ritual as she thought about her grandson. It was a big responsibility, but she was well prepared for its reawakening.

Ina or Mother had told her the same story, adding a song which her *até* or father sang when Ina finished the story. It was a beautiful song! This impressed her deeply.

For centuries a grandfather sang the song to his grandson, who would then sing it alone in the wilderness where no other ears could hear, except for the Creator. In the last four generations, however, there were no boys born, so a son-in-law was taught the song. He in turn passed it down to another son-in-law. This was no accident, as in the story, it was prophesied that there would be no male child born to the "honored" family. This, it was told, was a test of strength and faith for the nation as a whole. After four generations, and at least twenty years before the turn of the century, a boy would be born to the family. That son would be responsible for the Turn of the Century ceremony.

Wichaxpi was told that in life, people, places, and events change. Some changes are slow in coming; some are fast; however, certain things cannot and must not be changed. Her story is one that could not be changed. The story had to be enacted as told; the prayers, the songs and the ritual objects could not be changed. It was how her people stayed connected to their past generations.

Chapter 2

Nigxesancincala Fawn

Everyone was prepared: everyone included the female line of the last Kiktopawingxa, down through time, the story retold, a song kept alive without change in words or tune, for a millennium. Khugyuhamaniwin in turn told it to her daughter, Wichaxpi, who now held the boy-child in her arms.

The new mother thought of her unci as she lay gazing at her son. At dawn, an initiation ceremony would take place. The *eyapaha* or town crier would come and announce the beginning of the event. At the break of dawn, the baby's father would step outside the lodge with his son wrapped only in a softened deerskin. The oldest man in camp would have the honor of singing the special initiation song to introduce an old soul to the universe, a Kiktopawingxa to the rising sun.

The child's grandmother said to her husband, "What will we teach him first?" "Who will teach him first?" Unci knew that the work set before them would not be easy. "Where do we begin?" she murmured as she fell asleep.

She dreamt about the group of stars called "Chinshka"; her responsibility to her daughter was revealed to her. The first star was a sign to introduce her *txakozha* or grandson to the universe. One by one, the other stars signified important rituals for boys and girls. There were a total of eight stars in this constellation. Seven stars made the outer shape, and at its center lay a grandmother star, called Txowin.

Khugyuhamaniwin told her of other star patterns, including one called "Ochethi Yamni Teepeela" or Three Fires. She showed Wichaxpi the star map that had been in the family for many generations. Before passing it on to her daughter, she must tell of the constellations and their significance to the ritual. It must be assured that the daughter would not change words or leave out anything about the constellations.

The daughter then must learn to teach her son to paint the events of the night sky years from his birth. She must teach him to pass down the story, exactly as it had been told to her, as well as the song. He would then help teach parts of the story to his sister, who in turn must teach her daughter. How complex! All of this Khugyuhamaniwin was shown in her dream.

In the next teepee, Wichaxpi could not sleep. She lay gazing at her son, at his head, a soft black ball of fur, gently breathing while grasping her fingers, squeezing, letting go as he lay sleeping. He seemed to enjoy the freedom of moving, not knowing that by the end of the following day his little hands would be restricted, as he would be wrapped tightly, swaddled to develop a sense of calm in him.

She thought of the ceremony, the quill lizard pouch, the ear piercing ritual … all his firsts. She was getting far ahead of herself and quickly returned her thoughts to the moment, to the first major event to take place in the life of her son. She fell asleep knowing that soon, he would be introduced to the universe—at the rising sun.

Such were the events that began the life of Kiktopawingxa—or Kikto, as he was to be called.

Unci, Grandmother, knew that the work set before them would not be easy. The buffalo hide containing the star chart was fading; the painted constellations were fading. However, the names were not forgotten. The most important story for this Turn of the Century ceremony was the return of Wichaxpi Luta. The appearance of the red star brought new medicines for the people. New medicine would produce on the earth a new era, and a cleansing had already begun, with the appearance of the new grass. A more peaceful summer was to follow.

In the same constellation as the newly appearing red star, three other stars were always visible. The holy men high atop the mountains and those down on the Plains knew of these cleansing stars. It was to them that the truth was revealed. Star maps were painted on wolf hides and transported from the Plains below to the holy men atop the mountain and back again. This is how the holy men kept in communication. All of this the newborn baby boy had to be taught.

The Turn of the Century ceremony had been taking place for centuries unknown; the buffalo-hide maps of the stars and constellations told the story. In addition, certain cave walls told of the circle of rocks called *Inyan Kahomni* or Rock Circles. The maps showed where the circle of rocks was located. It was told that two such places could be located in underground cave walls. One place was near where a crazy woman lived long ago. The other caves were in the *Xe Sapa* or Black Mountains, the sacred place from which we came to be in this present world.

Unci was lamenting! Grandfather reminded her that there were many in her family that were trained to teach the boy. Everything would be all right. Were they not up late at nights gazing at the stars, looking for that special sign? Was it not true that each of the daughters were watched closely to see which would grow big around the stomach? Who was outside with them each time? The sign, he reminded her, was not only in the stars, but also a mark on the newborn baby.

So it began with the boy, Kikto, a happy child, bearing the mark that indicated his right to participate in ceremonial life and guide others, to ensure that the next generation would reach another millennium and return to this place to perform the ritual so rightfully belonging to the *oyate* or people.

When the boy started talking, he would recognize people. An old soul, he would tell their name and kinship. Soon, he lost interest as he began to play with other children. He did seem to possess some prior knowledge about making items boys were expected to make, those that helped remind them of their life responsibilities, to protect and to provide. It was essential to their very being, to learn early in life the importance of making those items and the specific value attached to each one.

Kitko's first such item was a slingshot, to kill small prey such as birds, rabbits, and other edible animals, for his mother and grandmother. He succeeded, but he was very sad about killing an animal, a rabbit. He could not join in the feast, but tradition told him he should. So he ate the rabbit with his family and others who were invited. His grandfather announced the first kill. All who attended applauded.

His next item was a spear. The mountain people speared fish, and they traveled down to the rivers and lakes to spear their fish. Although the boy was interested in hunting and spearing, he was not interested in war, nor was he encouraged to be.

His first *waniyapi* or pet was an orphaned raccoon. The mother was killed by accident. She was mistaken for a male and killed for her blood. Every part of her had to be utilized. Her two babies were saved and brought to Kikto, as people knew of his heart toward animals. In life there is a purpose for everyone and everything, and the male raccoon's blood had to be used to read the future.

His grandfather told him that at certain times, all female animal lives were spared, no matter how hungry a family might be, because they had little ones to care for. The young animals might not be able to survive on their own, because they had not yet learned how to take care of themselves. Therefore, when one was accidentally killed, the human beings had to look for the young and bring them home to raise until they could go away on their own.

His second pet was a dog, to become his friend and to learn to carry his belongings. Kikto also had to learn to properly tie the drags for his travels. In addition, his dog also learned his habits. In this way, they would be able to take care of each other.

A few years later, his grandfather caught a young male pronghorn. Kikto was to keep it for his pet. This animal he was expected to train, and he had to learn to be away from camp with it. His grandmother knew that all the years of their teachings would now be tested as this animal matured. The antelope would bring the boy to live alone as he followed it, taking care of it and later the herd that the antelope would bring to him. This would teach the boy to study the habits of the animals and birds, as well as the water and other elements of the earth. Most of all, he had to learn the constellation or the patterns in the night sky, our star relatives.

The male antelope began to grow horns. In the fall of the following year, he left to return to his wilderness home. In spring, the antelope would return, but he would not be alone. Winter followed and spring arrived, bringing the antelope home. He coaxed Kikto to follow him to a plum thicket where a doe and her fawn lay. The doe was shy but did not flee. She seemed to feel safe with the male nearby. The doe was standing and below her the fawn lay, almost unseen.

The boy was happy. His four-legged friend had returned with a family! He ran all the way back to the village, yelling for Grandmother and Grandfather. Grandmother was saddened by the turn of the events, but Grandfather was just as excited, for this was the beginning of the reason Kikto was born.

The village men were also excited. It was now time to take Kikto to the mountaintop, to that circle of rocks. The men wondered who would have the honor of taking the boy high up the mountain. This was just the beginning! Grandfather chose four wise and mature men, who were still young enough to travel. Four scouts were picked to guide the travelers. A ceremony must take place before they left for the mountains.

Their camp was close to the circle of rocks. They were at least a half a day's walk from it. The camps closer to the circle were mostly elderly people, men and women. The women were older but able-bodied women who knew of the sacred ways. They were no longer visited by "Unci," as they called the moon. In life, there was a time for everything.

It was time for this child's life purpose to begin. It was time to take the buffalo-hide map to the top of the mountain. The boy was thinking, *All this fuss when I can take it up to the mountain alone!* But deep in his heart, he knew that this trip was important to the people.

That evening the sacred fire was lit; cedar boughs were burned, and the smell was soothing and refreshing. There was an unusually deep silence in the village, as it was when sacred events were to take place. It seemed that even the children and dogs were especially quiet.

The boy, who had been sitting near the fire, stood and walked to the edge of the village, where the silence seemed to be deeper. He stood under the twinkling stars, listening as the waves of silence washed over him, cleansing him. He felt as if he were one with the universe. This was the first time he connected with his antelope; he knew where the antelope was, just as he stood at the edge of camp. It was his first such experience. He felt a deep love in his heart. He realized then how special his life purpose was. At that moment, the boy committed himself to his purpose, giving fully of himself, to complete it, no matter what it took, until it was fulfilled.

He realized that it would take some years. However, his youth and innocence helped him. He would do his part to the utmost, but as grandfather always said, "With your feet touching the earth!" to remind him that he was an *ikce wichasha*, a common man.

His name, Kiktopawingxa, was the third in his family from his mother's blood. His responsibility was to learn the song that Turn of the Century song and to read the stars, to know the constellation and its origin. In life's way, there were such boys, trained from infancy to learn Turn of the Century songs. He had to learn the song in order to teach another young man. This singer would be one of the assistants in the Turn of the Century ceremony.

His ancestral grandfather was a Kiktopawingxa. His name spoke of vast ages and keepers of the sacred songs. In his bloodline Kikto was the third such person to be so named, it was at least two thousand years ago that the song was first sung in his mother's bloodline. There was a hundred-year song, kept by each of the three Council Fires. His being present made him aware, though, that it had been a thousand years since the band had the honor of singing the song.

The seasons passed. It was near the time when Wichaxpi Luta was to appear. Kikto, now older, sat high atop a butte gazing at the herd of antelopes as they grazed. He looked closely at each one to determine how many would be traded, later this summer.

It is the belief of the nation that when one killed an animal, all of its parts were used. The hide was fashioned into clothes, moccasins, gloves, shields, and various bags. The bones were used similarly, to make snowshoes and sleds for winter. The meat went for drying and roasting, and some might even drink the blood, right after the kill, while it was still warm and bubbling. If they waited too long, the blood was not good to drink. In addition they ate the liver, kidneys, and heart when still warm. All of this was considered healthy for one's blood and overall health. Parts not suitable for people were fed to the dogs. Even internal organs were not overlooked: a bladder made a water bag, and a stomach was useful for making soup or served as a container.

The sun was now lowering to the west, as he decided to bring his herd to a nearby water hole and bed there for the night. He was happy that he had made himself a new flute; otherwise he would have to look for that special blade of grass to play music for his sweetheart, wherever she might be. He had not met her yet, but he knew that he would when it was time. He felt it in his heart, but in his mind he was not yet ready. The stars told him that until he fulfilled his responsibility to the oyate or nation, he could not take a wife. He sat near the water hole, under the shining stars, and played his flute, knowing that *kxate* or the wind carried the music to her heart. At last he put his flute away and lay gazing up at the stars. He pondered that the brightest twinkling stars were some of the ancestors who resided there after their final time in the physical world. He slept.

He was awakened by a nudge from his pack dog. He listened for unfamiliar sounds. However, before he saw the shadows, as it was just daybreak, he felt the vibration of the earth. His grandfather, Watxoye, Makes Blue, had told him about the buffalo run.

In the spring of each year, if one was lucky and at the right spot, one could see the buffalo running north at a fast pace. Grandfather told him that the buffalo did not stop until near sundown, only to run again the next morning. It was almost like a ritual for the buffalo, he was told. He had heard that the dust raised from this run could be seen for miles!

Buffalo were not good to eat until after their run. Usually in late summer and early fall, they were good to eat and their hides perfect for tanning. His grandfather told him that the buffalo ran to refresh their blood, from the long winter rest. Even people must run to refresh their blood, grandfather said; even the winged ones fly across the sky from sunup to midday and again for the rest of the day. In this way they, too, travel north.

Grandfather told him that where the first group of buffalo came there would be three or four more groups following in that same day. This would go on for many days, because the buffalo were countless!

Soon it would be time to begin preparing for the next winter. At the time of preparation the *thiyoshpaye* or extended families would break out into groups to hunt and gather at their favorite hunting places. These families were called that because they consisted of at least four generations of a family and sometimes other relatives. They would go to a place where the men would hunt, while the women and children would dig turnips and gather fruits. They followed certain trails that led to these places, sometimes wandering far away from their original camp.

It was here at these temporary camps that storytelling took place each night. The women would tell women stories; the men, hunting and war stories. Storytelling occurred in all villages at night. There were stories for night time and stories for day time.

Kiktopawingxa loved these stories, as many were about the stars and constellations. It was the medicine men or women who told some of the sacred star lore, pointing to the constellations. Each pointed out the stars that formed the constellations as they told their stories.

Chapter 3

Anpo Olowan, Sunrise song

Soon he would find such a camp. Dawn was breaking on the eastern horizon, leaving him to his prayers and the sunrise song. Everyone had to learn the sunrise song, it was absolutely necessary to sing this song each and every morning. If the women should find themselves alone in camp, one had to sing the song.

At times grandmothers were known to sing the sunrise song, because most men were out either hunting or at war. The old men present were unable due to voice loss or too weak to walk out to a spot to sing.

Kikto prayed, sang, washed his mouth, and ate some *wasna*, a dried mixture of meat, berries, and buffalo fat. Normally eaten for breakfast, it was also good travel food for any time of the day. He whistled for the leader of the herd. He hoped the leader would come out without delay, as he wanted to be across the prairie where the buffalo had run the day before.

The leader appeared, with the rest of the herd following. The sun was not yet hot. He knew he would be farther away by the end of the day. He crossed where the buffalo had run. The smell of buffalo sweat was strong.

As he climbed a ridge, he was able to see all around him. The mountains were a gorgeous silhouette of smoky blue. To the east he could see the tops of three buttes. He knew they were at least two or three days' journey from Xe Sapa, the Black Mountains—two or three days according to the herd. They took their time, grazing as they wandered the prairies. They seemed to have no care in the world. One thing he liked about them was that they were able to care for themselves and aware of their snake relatives. Kikto liked this time of the year, as the herd wandered far out onto the prairies. They grazed following a trail going down to a river.

In the spring the people made a seasonal migration toward the prairies and beyond. The thiyoshpaye journeyed in the different directions to where their relatives lived. These people followed the paths of their ancestors down the mountains they called *Xe Ska*. It was these trails or paths that the herd followed.

Now, in early spring, the herd led Kikto to an area where they said a crazy woman lived, in an underground cave near a river they named Crazy Woman. The cave was near the river, at an *okhizhata*, a fork in the river. Near the cave stood some tall rocks; her home, the tale went, was deep underground. One story told of a young man who became lost in the cave and was found wandering in a state of confusion near the Xe Ska. How he got there nobody knew..

When the people moved off the mountains toward the prairies, they cautioned their young men and women about this place. However, the *kxoshkalaka* (young men) and *wikxoshkalaka* (young women) would dare each other to go to this place at night. It was said the woman appeared at night. They would sneak away into the night to go to the cave.

They say the Crazy Woman could be heard crying, *"Omakiya, omakiya!"* But as soon as someone went into the cave to help her, she appeared as a red light, leading them deeper into the earth, where, if she took them deep enough, they would not be seen again. When the young people went down into the cave, they would stay together. They never really went deep, just far enough so they could still see the sky and the stars.

It was a clear night as Kikto lay thinking of this area and what the old people said. As he lay gazing at the stars, a group to the southeast began twinkling brighter and brighter; to the north another group of stars began twinkling. It looked as if they were communicating with each other, sending messages back and forth.

Some of the twinkling stars were parts of constellations, different from each other. As he lay watching the stars, thinking how close they seemed—almost as if he might reach up and touch one—suddenly a moving star appeared from the east, moving quickly across the sky toward the north. It passed a little east of overhead, dragging a flaming tail. He watched until it went out of sight.

He thought more about the stars and how his grandmother once told him about how the two-legged had four lives, and in each lifetime they had to accomplish something. Sometimes they would realize that they were in the fourth time, and then they would live their life right. At the end of that life, they would become a star, to watch over people eternally. He wondered about his own life and the great honor and responsibility given to him. He thought of his vision as well.

Another dawn arrived. He had forgotten about the crazy woman. Kikto was faithful to his rituals. Today he followed his herd into a ravine that took them to a cool spring where they drank the sweet water and grazed on the lush green grass. Kikto decided to paint a picture of him and his herd along the wall opposite the spring.

As he painted, he thought of the name given to such water holes, *wiwila*. A wiwila was considered to be a sacred place, inhabited by little men who could foretell one's future. Most of the time, childless couples would come to such a place to lie along the water's edge and gaze into the water until they saw their future with or without children. He had heard of couples who were childless who came to the spring only to go away disappointed.

On another day, he wandered with his herd, following them, taking care so no harm could befall them. He protected them from hungry predators such as the *shungmanitu* and the *yashle*, the wolves or the coyotes. They arrived on a ridge that ended in a cliff above a river.

This river was flowing clear as the bright blue sky. He found a path that led downward. Loose black dirt was its trail bed. The leader hesitated. Kikto thought about the time it had taken to get here. To turn and go back would take a long time, perhaps half a day or longer. The choice was easy to make: they had nowhere to go but down. He grabbed the leader by his antlers and sat down, sliding them downhill on the loose dirt.

Kikto knew he had to swerve quickly to one side at his next chance. He rolled to the left, as the leader kept sliding. He dropped into a deep, cold river! His leader was already along the bank across the river, as the rest of the herd splashed their way across.

Kikto took advantage of the time. He knew he had to find a way to hike back to the top of the ridge to get his pack dog and belongings. His dog waited patiently, trusting his owner to come for him.

He found a trail that the pack dog could follow. It was easier to see from the bottom. He led his dog down this path; then, at he river, he removed the pack and let the dog swim across.

Kikto then found a place where he would nap in the sun, but later awaken in a shade. His dog curled up next to him. He lay there listening to the cottonwood leaves as they whispered to each other. *Beware of Ikto*, they seemed to say; *he is always near*. He heard birds singing and bees buzzing and could see the butterflies landing softly here and there. *All life is busy*, he thought as he drifted off to sleep.

"Thiblo, thiblo!" cried the bird, who was once a two-legged, in search of her older brother. The cries awakened him. He went for a swim and decided to spend the night. He fixed his *thiyokthi* or small willow hut and put his belongings inside. He then went back out to the shallow part of the river to catch a *hosapa*, a catfish.

He dug a shallow hole in which he layered some rocks and built a fire. He cleaned the fish and packed the meat in mud, which he laid over the now glowing rocks until the mud was dried and cracked. He removed it from the fire and waited for it to cool a little. His dinner was fresh fish with a little melted buffalo fat. He enjoyed his meal.

Soon after he finished his dinner, it was dark. He went to his hut. Some wild deer had come down to the river to drink. They kept glancing his way; clearly they sensed his presence, but he sat very still and tried to breathe quietly. The deer drank and left for the prairies.

That night he awakened to the barking and howling of the *shungmanitu txanka*, the timber wolves. It seemed as if they were teaching their young to bark and howl; fascinated, he could hear echoes of young timber wolves as the adults called again and again. Soon, however, he heard a reply far above them, toward the ridge they had descended earlier in the day.

He thought about his herd—where had they gone? Did they follow the river? In the morning he would follow their tracks. The antelope loved some of the spring flowers that bloomed at this time of year.

They especially loved the sunflowers. They ate the whole plant, from the flowers to the stem. They also loved the young sweet clovers, as did Kikto, who often ate the yellow flowers.

His life purpose came into his thoughts. He had to be at a certain place by this time next spring and return to the mountains by fall. He wondered about the first person it was prophesied that he would meet, one of the five helpers he would eventually encounter. As he pondered, another thought distracted him.

His grandfather said that long ago, there were many rivers in which the waters flowed from bank to bank. Grandfather said that at such places dwelled water people who were considered sacred. These water people spoke of future events and events of the stars and the universe. They were careful about who they chose to speak to. Some men and women, Grandfather said, would go to such rivers to speak to the water people, but the water people, knowing the seekers' insincerity, would not come out of the water. The seekers who came forgot that the Creator put everything upon the earth and sky and in between for the two-legged. All the seekers wanted was to gain or acquire knowledge to fool the ignorant people for self-gain.

That night, as he lay gazing at the moon, a lonely cloud slowly drifted across. He knew the moon would soon be full; he had developed the habit of keeping track of its phases. He also counted the days in between on a stick that was made especially for that purpose.

His counting the phases of the moon was different from the women's way of counting, he was told. The women watched the moon for a different purpose. They also watched for the appearance of certain stars to know when to plant their gardens, when to dig for food, and when they should not go near food or handle food. One of the uses for counting the moon helped in delivering their children.

As he mused on all this, his thoughts returned to the day he was first taken up to the mountains to get his set of instructions. He was taken to the circle of rocks where the holy men continually studied the events of the stars, sleeping during the day and counting the passing of the moon. His journey, the one he was on, began immediately after he was given instructions. He was told not to go directly to his destination. He was told that herd would lead him in the right direction. Instead of turning them back toward the mountains, he was to follow them and not to turn back, only to continue his eastward journey.

At the time of his instructions, he was living high up in the mountains where his people had camped for the winter. Part of the land was flat, and there was plenty of wood and water. He now thought of the place he was being taken. There, high in the mountains, were two circles of rocks; the larger one was near a ridge where the land was flat. The smaller was toward the southeastern part on a higher hill or a butte. It was from this butte that the stars were studied. The larger circle of rocks is where the sacred Turn of the Century ceremony was to be held.

Kikto thought of the main group of stars that he was to study each night. He was instructed on how to detect the sign that would take him on his journey and to continue to recognize the same sign in the different ways that it would appear. The holy men on the mountain instructed him on this and other ways that he would need to know.

Kikto set off from the top of the mountain a few days after the villagers had taken him there. He was patient; he knew this was one of the virtues he must practice. Also, he had many moons to return to this mountain at a certain time. He was allowed plenty of time to do this. It was dawn; he sang the sunrise song and ate.

He had journeyed most of the day carrying his bladder-bag of water and his pack dog. His plan was to reach the Xe Sapa by the next day. He continued on the trail he had been following. If anyone should meet him, traveling alone like that, they would think of him as one of the outcasts and stay away from him.

His style of dress, however, did not resemble that of the outcasts. His *chegnaka* or breechcloth still had its buffalo hair on the outside, with the inside softened. He carried his walking stick, which did not resemble those carried by leaders. There were no feathers at the tip of the stick. It did have a small piece of buffalo hair wrapped at the holding spot.

Kikto was about eighteen winters. Before he left his village, the people had a feast for him, as he would not be returning for at least two winters. It was then that his grandmother told him of how many winters he would be and that by the time he returned, the ceremony would take place. At that time he would have two more winters of experience in his life.

Grandmother told him of his initiation ceremony at that time. It had been only a few days since then, yet it seemed like such a long time ago! Kikto had witnessed the initiation of newborn boys. He participated in one where the infant was believed to be an old soul returning, said to be a strong and fearless warrior.

As the chosen man prayed for this particular child, he asked for blessings for a strong and brave warrior, with sharp eyes and keen ears, capable of making good choices and understanding the visible and invisible, should he someday become a leader of his nation.

As the speaker began singing, Kikto thought of his own life. He wondered if he had this vision, the ability to understand the visible and the invisible. He gazed at the now fading stars as the song ended.

The infant was faced to the sun, front and back, then turned in four directions as the sun rose. At the end of this ceremony, some women sang a brave heart song and trilled. Women would honor such an infant, knowing they were getting older and the infant might be their provider from time to time. Kikto had been thinking about this ceremony as he walked.

He arrived at a village near Matxo Paha or Bear Butte. He knew its legend, he recognized the stars above it, and he knew the significance of the stars to the circle and to the people. According to the legend this is the place where the two-legged and four-legged first lost communication. Before that time they were able to talk to each other. It is was where the two-leggeds were given instructions on how to take care of the living things and the earth itself.

He had arrived in the early evening, as storytelling was about to start. The sun had just gone beyond the western horizon. Some of the younger children were asleep. Some were still awake, ready to listen to perhaps their favorite stories. Storytelling was a favorite time for all.

Chapter 4

Ohunkankan: Storytelling

Kikto, having just arrived, was tired and decided to sleep tonight and listen the following night. He awoke at dawn, in the Plains, where the light of day meets the edge of night pushing it away, a time when the stars seem to be dancing brightly, sparkling reds, blues, and yellows promising to return soon. Soon the sky lightens in hues of red, orange, and yellow as the sun rose.

It was at that moment that he heard the men in the village sing an initiation song. Kikto witnessed the whole event. He was happy, for soon he would be eating food cooked by women. He would join the celebration of life, happy that he had arrived when he did.

He had camped at the edge of the village—the traditional way, unless someone invited you to sleep as their guest. As morning advanced, the whole village came alive with activities leading toward the coming feast. The feast would be finished before the sun rose high in the sky. The children played, shouting and laughing; barking dogs joined the merriment.

Kikto walked to the river, where he had seen the tops of black heads disappear. When he arrived at the river he dipped his toes in the water to find it warm, unlike the cold swimming places in the mountains.

He knew the river. It was the river he had crossed somewhere upstream the day before . The river flowed in a northerly direction to meet another river that flowed from the northeast. Where two rivers meet is called okhizhata or a fork in the rivers.

There is a place called *okhizhata washté* or beautiful fork. The reference is to the surrounding area, which is beautiful. The rivers flowed clear and freely. That place, Kikto knew, was nearby.

It was told that the land there was magnificent. Trees thick with green leaves supplied ample shade, the river provided a deep swimming hole, and various flowers grew everywhere! The scent of night-blooming flowers, it was said, filled the air all around. The night birds could be seen on moonlit nights. After the rain, his mother said, the mushrooms were the best. She had tasted the mushrooms. He didn't remember tasting mushrooms, but for sure his mother had.

She told him that when he was still on a cradle board, they had camped there and stayed nearly the whole summer. She told him that it was her wish that someday he would take his own son, while still on a cradle board, and stay a few days..

As he thought of this, he was knee deep in the river. He continued walking toward the deeper part lifting his chegnaka, eventually taking it off and tossing it up on the river bank. Soon he immersed himself in the water and began swimming.

The older boys wanted to have a swimming race. Two of them immediately swam to opposite directions to be the beginning and end markers, for the now anticipated race. A few older boys, more his age, arrived.

As a young child, Kikto was a loner, preferring to play alone. In his village that was acceptable, due to his life purpose. Today, he allowed himself to enjoy the festivities, lest people think him strange.

Two younger boys started the races, cheered on by friends and relatives. The object was to go touch the boy farther away and return to the starting point and touch that boy, thus winning the race. All of the races involved two swimmers. At last the groups finished. At this point, a young man arrived, and everyone cheered as they challenged Kikto to race him.

Kikto saw that they were about the same height and built. He took the challenge, and as he got into position, he imagined himself already touching the farther boy and returning to touch the first boy. As he swam, he imagined himself racing his lead antelope. He did not notice that all the cheers had died down; it was very quiet, except for the splashing of the water as they raced. As he touched the first boy again, the other swimmer was right behind him.

He had been given Iyeshni, Doesn't Speak, to race. Up until today, Iyeshni had never been defeated in a swimming contest, but Kikto had done so in a most graceful manner. Those who watched the race saw that the two racers had calm about their faces as they raced. This would be the talk of the summer!

Other races followed but none as good as the one between Iyeshni and Kikto. There were adults standing at the banks of the river, watching. Soon after they had finished, Iyeshni's father invited Kikto to come to their lodge for the feast. He accepted.

The feast was to honor the family of the newborn boy. It was a tradition that had been held for centuries. The family was invited to come to the center of the village; *"Chokata ú po!"* was the eyapaha's invitation as he called the honored family. A song was sung for the family, all sat in a circle and gifts were brought for the child.

During the time when everyone was eating, an elderly woman called the eyapaha to her teepee, sending a grandson to get him. When he arrived, she told him they had a distinguished guest amongst them. A young man destined to do the Turn of the Century ceremony. Had he recognized him?

The eyapaha had been so busy the night before that he did not recognize the young man. The eyapaha was curious as to how an older woman who had never left the village recognized this young man. Kikto's presence marked another element of the prophecy yet to be told.

Lechel oyake: She told it like this, a woman relative of the honored family would meet Kikto near to the time of the ceremony. In this meeting there would another boy, one who did not speak—Iyeshni. This boy would become one of the helpers to the ceremony. There would be five young men, she was told as a young girl in another village by her unci. As she finished telling the eyapaha, she went inside her teepee and cried. The unci who had told her this was now gone, yet her words had come true this very day!

Kikto, unaware, sat eating with his new friend, Iyeshni. There was a persistent tugging at his memory. He knew it was connected to Iyeshni, but what was it? He could not remember. Suddenly a bird chirped, and he thought of his herd. It was impolite to leave in the middle of a meal, so he waited. Soon Iyeshni's father had finished eating. He grabbed some fine dirt and rubbed it between his hands to wash off the fat. He stood, stretched, and yawned; he would go to his teepee to lie down.

Kikto motioned to Iyeshni to follow him as he informed the boy's father that he would go to the nearest butte to look for his herd. Iyeshni's father showed him which butte the scout was watching. The father motioned for Iyeshni to take Kikto to the scout's butte.

It was a beautiful place. It was high, giving a good view of a large area of the land. As they stood, Kikto was impressed by the circular horizon. The smell of pine enhanced the beauty, leaving him somewhat dreamy. He had not smelled the pine forest since he left the mountains; however, this pine scent was different, strikingly fresh.

The scout told Kikto that he had spotted a herd of antelope, pointing out the direction. The herd had filed down the western slope of a butte not very far from them. Kikto knew that it was his herd and that for some reason the leader was keeping them in the valley. Kikto was not the only antelope herder; there were many, including some out in the Plains. When hunters saw that the antelope were in herds, they knew that the owner was nearby somewhere.

Kikto knew he would give a *makhicima*, a lean one, to the family of the newborn. At the moment he decided this, the tugging in his heart came to light. In his prophecy, he would meet one of the helpers at the place where he gave one of his antelopes to a newborn boy. He was told his helper would be an unusual person, although they did not tell him in what way he would be marked.

He would be the first helper Kikto would meet at the beginning of the preparation for the ceremony. With that thought, Kikto turned to look at Iyeshni. Iyeshni had a puzzled look on his face, as if he, too, knew, but he could not verbalize what he knew; he could only sign. This was deep, they both knew. A sense of excitement filled the air, and for a moment the two young men seemed to communicate in thought only.

The scout watched them as they seemed to have some kind of silent communication. The scout broke the silence by asking if the feast had taken place yet. Kikto told him that it had. Soon another scout would come to replace him, and he was hungry.

Kikto began walking toward where the herd had been spotted. Iyeshni followed. He found the herd, but they were spooked a little by Iyeshni. Kikto looked over all of them, choosing the one he would present to the family. He tied a strip of leather and led her away toward the village.

As they neared the village, he sent Iyeshni, who knew this tradition, to seek the eyapaha, who would announce the gift for the child. The father would then come to take the gift. Iyeshni did his part, and soon the father came to accept the gift. Some women accompanied him and helped with the skinning and preparation of the meat and hide. Dogs eagerly awaited their share.

The hottest time of day had passed, and soon the festivities would resume. In anticipation of the coming dance, people prepared themselves by painting their faces and donning the best of their dress. They prepared to do the 'grand entry' or *ikpazo wachipi*. Such festivities took place under the sun. Although they had waited for day to cool, the sun was still high in the sky. There was time.

Ikpazopi, it was called, everyone dressed in their finest, painted their faces according to tradition and their place in life, dreams, and visions. It was time to show off the best of their clothing, their quilling and painting skills. Most of the clothes were being worn for the first time. The new items included entire outfits—dresses, leggings, hair pieces, and the painting. Some came from dreams and some from visions.

They parted and braided their hair, painting the parted section of their head. Each had its own significance. On their face paint the women used yellow, while the men used red. Each individual had its own significance. When everyone was ready, the eyapaha began with a prayer. All faced the west first, then turned toward the north, east, and finally the south. At this point all were facing the normal direction, to the center where the eyapaha stood. As he finished, the singing began.

The singers who were already at the center each had a drum; they pounded in unison and sang the Coming to the Center song. Everyone participated, all except the elderly, who could not go out to the center. Infants were on cradle boards on the backs of their mothers. They came into the center with the elderly men leading the women and children in, followed by the older boys and men. For Kikto it was exciting.

The group entered from the west entrance, and the men who were leading now danced to the right of the circle, while the women and children began dancing to the left. Soon, all the women and children had formed an inner circle, with the men and older boys dancing in the opposite direction in an outer circle. The song was sung until all dancers had made four complete circles.

Then the singing stopped, and the eyapaha called the honored family and the infant to the center. The honored family came out with their child swaddled tightly in a cradle board. On one side stood the father and his family, and on the side, the mother and her family. All came to embrace the child. It was in such a way that the newborn was honored.

Kikto wondered if his celebration was similar. He approached the sleeping child and put his hands over the cheeks, the palms first then the backs of both hands on both cheeks of the child. He felt an overwhelming sensation he had never felt before. Behind him more people followed.

More dancing followed, soon it would be time for *ohunkankan* or nighttime storytelling. As the honoring was now done, everyone went home to change into their regular clothing. No one washed off the paint on the part in their hair, out of consideration for the ancient ones who came to visit, so they might recognize them by the paint.

It was now dark, and ohunkankan would soon begin. Some children who were tired were asleep already, but others were awake and ready to listen. Under the twinkling stars an old man began his story. He told of how the four-legged, the two-legged, the winged ones, and many other small creatures once had a race. For four days and nights they raced. The earth vibrated as they raced, and dust filled the air.

The first day, he said, one animal died, his spirit rose up to become a star, and a butte near where he fell was named after him. On the second day, another animal died; he likewise became a star, and the butte near where he fell was named after him. Over the course of the first four days, five animals died and became stars, and five buttes were named after them. He pointed to each star and then lowered his arm toward the earth to locate each butte and say its name.

The five stars in the sky and the five buttes on the earth, he concluded, were there to remind the two-legged of their responsibility as stewards of the earth from that time on. Many men agreed aloud; "Hau, hau, hau," could be heard from all directions.

A second man began the story of how Matxo Paha, Bear Butte, came to be. He told of how children were out berry picking when a bear chased them. The boys told the girls to remain in a certain spot while they ran for help. The girls prayed so hard that the Creator took pity on them and made the earth beneath their feet grow. As the earth rose upward, the hungry bear scratched all around, leaving the sides with deep claw marks. That is why the butte looks as it does to this day. Again, "Hau! Hau! Hau!" could be heard all around. It meant that the story was true to form.

Another man told a story about the stars, eliciting a chorus of agreement among the listeners. The children remained silent, listening, for they were hearing some the stories for the first time. They would listen again and again until they were able to tell the story as the storytellers were now doing. At that time, they, too, would agree or disagree in unison.

Next a woman stood and said she wanted to tell a woman's star story. She told of how two girls who were *mashké* or sister-friends, chose star husbands. These girls, she related, were childhood friends. They have been friends from the time they could walk and talk. One was very beautiful, while the other was homely.

The homely girl asked the pretty one which star she would choose for her husband. The beautiful girl gazed at the stars until she spotted a bright twinkling star and said, "That one, that one will be my husband." The storyteller pointed to a star as she continued the story.

The homely girl looked around near the bright star. She spotted a dim red star and pointed to it, saying, "I will marry that one so I can stay close to you." They fell asleep and woke up to their star husbands.

The beautiful girl was married to a handsome young man with thick black braids. He was a good hunter. He told her she could dig for edible plants but not the *tinpsila*; which was forbidden.

Likewise, her friend awakened to a star husband. He was an older man with braided gray hair. He was also a good hunter and provider. He, too, told his wife that she might dig of edible plants, all but the tinpsila. They lived on the stars for a time.

One day the pretty girl decided she would dig the tinpsila. She dug a hole on the star that allowed her to look down at the earth and became very homesick, after seeing their village. She summoned her friend, and together they braided ropes using the stem and roots of the tinpsila along with other materials to make rope. They made a long rope to climb down to earth.

At this time both girls were going to have babies. The beautiful girl went down first. She fell and died, but her baby lived. Next the other girl jumped from the end of the rope and found her friend had died, while her baby was alive. Her own baby had died after her fall. She wrapped her baby and put her in the arms of her friend. She laid them nicely, planning to return later with her family. She took her friend's baby and set out to find her village.

A meadowlark that had been watching now spoke to the surviving girl. The meadowlark told her that she knew where to find their village. The homely friend now followed the meadowlark, who was taking her home.

Upon returning to her village, she told her unci about the things that had happened, explaining about the baby and wanting to know where her friend's parents now camped.

Together they went to the teepee of her friend and told her family what had happened. They all agreed that she would keep the baby. The baby began crawling the next day. He grew quickly, and the following day he was walking. They named him Wichaxpi Hokshila or Star Boy.

Star Boy became a strong warrior, hunting for two families, and took care of the poor. From that time many stories were told of his bravery and generosity. Men and women acknowledged the story in each their own way.

Kikto noticed that in this village at storytelling the men threw a pinch of tobacco, *chanshasha* into the fire before telling their story. He also noticed that when the woman got up to tell her story, it was the eyapaha who put chanshasha into the fire. Kikto would one day return home, and at that time he would pay closer attention to such matters. At that moment he could not recall the distinct smell of chanshasha or of it being used at storytelling in his village.

So ended the evening. Iyeshni invited Kikto to spend the night in his teepee, which he accepted gratefully. He knew there would be soft robes. He was right. That night he slept soundly.

All too soon it was morning. He decided to spend one more night to listen to more stories that night. He was awakened to the sunrise song. Finishing the song, the eyapaha yelled, "Kikta po! Anpa yelo!" (Wake up, it is daylight!) And a new day had begun.

Kikto went looking for his herd, with Iyeshni following close behind him. He sought a hill in the direction he had last seen them. While they were gone, the people in the village decided they should acknowledge his presence by honoring him.

When Kikto and Iyeshni returned, the eyapaha announced their return. Kikto was called to the center. "Kikto, chokata ú wo!" (Kikto, come to the center) was the invitation. He had no idea why he was being asked to come to the center. Perhaps the family to whom he had given the deer wanted to thank him in this way.

He recognized the oldest man of the village and his wife. They looked grand! The lines on their faces showed the wisdom they possessed, and the graying of their hair showed the many winters they had spent together. Soon others arrived.

Everyone sat in a circle with the men at the center. The leader sat before the people's staff. It had three feathers tied together at the top to represent the Three Nations. *Ochethi Yamni*, it was called. Behind him sat his family.

As more people arrived, Kikto thought about his grandfather. A sadness briefly crossed his heart. His grandfather had told him of the political aspects of the culture. To honor one who is not of the village, its leader must post the staff with the three feathers. He noted that this village followed tradition as Grandfather had explained.

At last the eyapaha sent his voice to the four winds, in accord with tradition, to begin the honoring ceremony. An honor song followed as all participants stood and danced in place as the eyapaha led Kikto with their hands raised high, dancing him in a circle for all to see the honored man. Some women trilled. Some men encouraged or *akish'ash'a* as Kikto was marched before them. He wondered why he was being so honored. Perhaps this village honored all their guests this way.

The song ended as the eyapaha announced: *"Mitakuyepi, anagxoptan po!"* Listen, my relatives! *"Kxoshkalaka ki le Watxoye thiyoshpaye etanhan yelo!"* This young man is from the Makes Blue Family. *"Kiktopawingxa heca yelo!"* He is the Kiktopawingxa!

Women trilled, "Lililili!," while the men yelled, "Hahahey!" To them it was a high honor to have such a one in their midst. It sent a chill through Kikto's body. He had never been honored in such a manner!

The eyapaha continued: "This young man is called Kikto; he is the one who will perform the Turn of the Century ceremony, on our most sacred mountain, Inyan Kahomni Xepxa."

At this point Kikto was expected to tell his story. As he told the story, he realized he needed to add his meeting with Iyeshni and the significance of their meeting. He wished his grandparents were here.

People got up and came to shake his hand. Some rubbed both sides of his arms at the same time; it was a sign of love. A sensational feeling went through his body. He remembered when his grandmother would rub his cheeks with the palms and backs of her hands. This brought back the same feeling of being loved, cared for, and honored. He recalled his grandmother saying, *"Unshikela,"* and it always made him feel like crying.

The honoring ceremony was over. Everyone went to their lodges, food had been plentiful, dancing was excellent, and storytelling was splendid. All this was on Kikto's mind as he drifted off to sleep.

He never forgot his nighttime gratitude prayer to the Creator. He thought about this as well. Why was it that one had to pray only three times a day? It did not seem enough for what was given to the two-leggeds. He certainly appreciated this and more.

At dawn, soon after the eyapaha sang the morning song, Kikto gathered his belongings in preparation for leaving. As he packed, he recalled the story from an elderly woman who was a cousin to his grandmother. The two had grown up together in another village far to the south. She announced that she would travel to Xe Ska to see her cousin, while she was still able to walk. They would spend a winter or two to await the coming ceremony.

Chapter 5

Iglaka: Moving Camp

It was time to leave. His journey would take him toward the east. His dog was waiting, packed and ready for travel. Kikto looked toward where his newest unci had camped. Her teepee was taken down in preparation for their travel to the west. A scout awaited them.

Two or three more teepees had been taken down. At least five lodges were leaving. They began their journey, talking and laughing as they moved away from this camp. Soon it would quiet down, as they walked silently. At some point they would sing a camp moving song. A food offering was taken to the base of the highest nearby butte, the one called Matxo Paha or Bear Butte, before they traveled.

Kikto sent a message to his grandparents and family. *"Ikxopxab shni yo, taku iyuha washté yelo."* Do not be afraid, everything is good. He did not say anything more, as he knew his unci would love for him to tell everything that had happened since he came to this camp. Truth was important to everyone.

"We must always tell the truth," his unci had told him many times as a young boy. He knew the new grandmother would not leave out any part of his sojourn at her camp. She would especially love to tell how she was the first to recognize him as part of the prophecy. Indeed, all things were going well.

The herd stayed in front of him, grazing as they moved onward as if in a hurry. He walked a bit faster than usual. Iyeshni walked along quietly.

He noticed an eagle flying above the herd. He had noticed that a few days ago, before he came to Iyeshni's camp. The eagle seemed to be watching over the herd, which was very unusual. They were now upon flatlands ascending from the creekbed they had been following. They could see far ahead and in all directions.

The land was hilly. Ascending was hard work; descending, one could see a vast land. It took a very long time to get from one hill to the next. In that way they traveled. As they topped each hill, the most exhilarating sight greeted them.

A high butte hidden behind the rolling hills stood proudly. All around the butte was grassless and treeless, bare dirt. One could see the results of where the rainwater flowed down the steep hillsides. He wondered how long it would take to get there.

A large herd of buffalo were grazing not far from the butte as they traveled past. Kikto soon realized that this was one of the sacred buttes. He wondered about its name as Iyeshni, seeming to sense the question, provided the answer. He motioned toward two small children about the same size, and then toward a teepee. Kikto offered, "Chekpa Teepeela!" Where Twins Dwell a sacred mountain. Iyeshni nodded in affirmation.

They followed a teepee drag trail (*ochanku*, they were called) leading in an easterly direction. Soon they came upon another river, where Iyeshni communicated by gestures that this was the same river in which they had first met. This was amazing to Kikto; so much had happened in that short time.

His grandfather had told him that the *wakpala* or creeks led to *mini hanska* or rivers, and mini hanska led to the larger rivers leading to the *mini wanca* or the ocean. His grandfather had gone to the ocean once when he was young, but as Kikto thought of this, he could not imagine his grandfather ever leaving their mountain home.

They followed the river in an easterly direction looking for a *cheyaktxun* or a *khiyuwegxa*, a bridge or a crossing. The ochanku they were following had taken a northerly direction, and they decided to abandon it. Instead they followed the path that Kikto's herd was now following; apparently they knew where they were going. The path was a migration trail for the deer, elk, and other four-leggeds. It led them to where the animals were able to swim across an okhiyuwegxa.

Some ways beyond the crossing, several logs lay across the narrow creek, as if some beavers had once made a home here. On the other side of the creek, the herd was running across the prairies, clearly loving the open space. They would soon be grazing nearby.

Kikto looked back to see Chekpa Teepeela standing proudly. He then wondered about the two doors, the entrance to the cave. Perhaps they were on the other side. His grandfather had told him about the doors. He said only those whose faith was strong could enter the cave.

They continued easterly as the sun traveled across the sky. *Wi wankatuya el*, at the sun's highest peak in the sky, it was also the hottest time of the day. At this point, they found a lone cedar tree where they decided to rest. Kikto offered a small pinch of tobacco at its base, following his grandfather's teachings and the core of his belief.

They slept. Upon awakening, Kikto saw Iyeshni returning with a rabbit. They would have fresh meat for their *xtawotapi* or evening meal. He skinned the rabbit and used his *isan* to section it. Iyeshni had built a fire for the roasting. Kikto remembered tasting this only once, when they were visiting relatives who lived in the south, Chasmu Oyate, they were called. He could remember the taste even today. He loved the taste of *mashtinca pxemnayanpi* or roasted rabbit.

They fed their dogs the entrails'. The dogs would not eat the rabbit's head, so the people found a small ant hill and left it nearby so the ants could eat. They took its hide and stretched it out to dry. It would take a day or two to dry. They left the hide there; people who were traveling who would make use of it.

They continued their journey eastward. There was plenty of daylight left for traveling. They walked along a creek for a while, soon leaving it to follow an animal migration trail that led upward on to the prairie.

They had stopped to camp for the night. Kikto looked back to the west, where he witnessed a spectacular sunset. Against the western horizon, Xe Sapa was silhouetted in glows of amber, red orange, and faint yellow streaks against a purplish sky. He did not realize he had been holding his breath until he exhaled. He had not seen anything like it before! He sat and watched it as it slowly faded into the western horizon.

He found a good spot to sleep for the night. The stars were announcing their presence all at once, it seemed. The sky looked very big to Kikto; it was different from the mountain sky. Some of the stars twinkled softly, while others remained red, blue, or a dim white color. The sky looked like it was dancing, alive, vibrant with life. Kikto was happy.

His grandfather told him that in the night there is life; one has to be there to observe. There were some flowers that bloomed in the night, and there were birds that visited the flowers for their food. People, he said, did not belong in the night. He said all things had their place and purpose. Therefore he said, "When you are traveling and happen to camp outside, respect this. Whatever it is that you see, observe and learn from it." As he lay there thinking about this, another thought came to him.

Echani ki, he thought, *soon we will be in that place known as Seven Sacred Springs, Wiwila Shakowin.* As children they were warned of little people that lived near these springs. One had to be careful not to encounter them. It was said that people there could sense they were being watched. Another story he remembered as he lay gazing into the night sky was the story of how a childless couple could go to one of the wiwila and peer into it together to see whether they would conceive.

When such a couple went to visit the wiwila, they went alone, approaching the wiwila from opposite sides and then lying down on their bellies across from each other to gaze into the water. Soon, it was said, one or more babies might appear. If none appeared, then they would be childless. For Kikto that was one of the mysteries of life. He fell asleep.

He was awakened by the smell of cedar and warm breath. His heart pumped hard, he was almost afraid to open his eyes. Kikto opened his eyes to his lead antelope's nostrils in his face! He yelled, *"Hanta yo!"* Get away! as he sat up. The rest of the herd was nearby grazing; they seemed to always be hungry. It was already daylight. He quickly did the morning song, wondering why he had slept so soundly. Iyeshni was gone; he must have awakened earlier.

Iyeshni found a small creek where he washed his face and rinsed his mouth. The water was bitter; *mini skuya*, it was called, bitter water, not fit for drinking. He returned to camp and motioned to Kikto about the water. He followed Kikto to the water; the pack dogs had followed waiting patiently to drink some of the water. Dogs didn't seem to worry about taste; they either just ate or just drank the water.

They continued their journey after eating a bit of the wasna their unci had packed for them. They journeyed up and down hills; in some places grass flowed like water, with butterflies fluttering from one prairie flower to the next. There was a place where they walked very carefully across a field of cactus that was abloom with flowers! Kikto was very impressed with nature and how things were created. He wondered about their purpose.

Iyeshni, ever the mind reader, stopped to show how to draw water from the cactus plants. He pulled one out by its roots, removed the roots, and buried them back where he had found the plant. He held the stem, which was not prickly, and twisted it. When that came off, he put his mouth on it, showing how he could drink the water. Kikto would ask Grandfather about the cactus when he returned to the mountains.

The trail they were following led them downward into a hilly region. As they descended they could smell the spring water and the tea that grew around the area. The tea, a mint tea, very good to drink, was called *cheyaka*. The leaves were left in a water bag all day long in the sun. At the evening meal the tea was shared.

As they descended, they realized they were in the area known as the Wiwila Shakowin, a sacred site. Kikto would remember the story. He had heard it. All people must know why sacred places were named as such. Whatever the story or where it began it would be told at storytelling somewhere. There was always someone who told the origins of such stories.

At the bottom was the first spring. There Kikto prayed with tobacco or chanshasha for a good journey, for understanding, and for things to always go right for him, for Iyeshni, and for those he had yet to meet. They made camp at the bottom. The seven springs they were all close together on the same draw, and the area was covered with fruits of all kinds, chokecherries, plums, currants, grapes, tea, and other edible plants. Kikto and Iyeshni were both curious about spending the night at a sacred site.

Before daylight faded away, the stars were becoming visible, twinkling in the sky, as Kikto noticed there seemed to be stars twinkling upon the earth as well. The fireflies or *wanyeca* were awake and darting here and there around the meadow of the spring. Some were near the water; others kept to the various bushes and along the stream that led from one spring to the next.

Kikto sat gazing at the wonderment of creation. How clever the Txunkashila or grandfather must have been to create such creatures! He lay in wonderment at this creation, on the earth and in the sky. He felt the need to sing a song from deep within his heart. It was a beautiful song! He sang it again, and this time from deep within he felt the need to cry. He did as he finished the song.

The next morning at dawn he awakened to the last of the visible stars and greeted the morning star with its song. He sang. It was a pleasant morning. They continued their journey downward. He followed the fresh tracks of his herd. They reached a barren valley, and as they did, he could smell the natural hot waters. A smell he knew from the hot springs near his mountain village. Both he and Iyeshni refreshed themselves by bathing in the natural hot water.

They smelled the campfires before they saw the teepees. They were now looking along a river or mini hanska. This river flowed from somewhere near the White Mountains or Xe Ska into the Muddy River or *Mini Shoshe*. Soon the camp came into view. There were children and dogs playing at along the river.

A garden stood proudly as they neared the camp. The eyapaha came to greet them. He asked where they were coming from and where they were going. He asked each one the names of their grandparents. This custom helped establish the larger family or *thiyoshpaye* people came from. There were many more questions as they reached the camp circle or *hochoka*.

Kikto wondered where their scout or *watuwan* were, he hadn't seen anyone since they had been traveling across the prairies. His grandfather warned him of enemy villages. The people in this village spoke his language. A strange dialect, but still the same language.

As Kikto spoke, the eyapaha announced the words. When he had finished, a young man near his age stepped forward, introducing himself. He had followed them for two days, he said. Kikto wondered why they had not seen him.

Grandfather was right: the people who dwelled in the prairies had some of the best scouts or watuwan. Grandfather had said, "If they want you to see them, they will show themselves. If not, then you may never see them." His thoughts came back to the present as they asked about Iyeshni.

It turned out that Iyeshni had relatives in this camp. They were invited to stay and given the guest teepee reserved for travelers or invited guests or *wichakichopi*, or guests of honor.

Kikto was most eager to hear the Ohunkankan. In many villages or camps there were interpreters for people like Iyeshni. He was happy that there was such a person here. Iyeshni was taken to the lodge of his relatives. Kikto was also invited. They were fed and told to rest.

Walking from sunrise to sunset was tiring but never boring, as there were many things to see and events that happened. On their journey a couple of days back they had seen two baby fox, *tokxala chincala*, sitting in the shade of their den or *igxugxa*. The rocks protruded out of the ground, stacked on top of each other upon the earth. These were red fox who dwelled in this sort of den.

As puppies they were cute and playful; however, it was best not to disturb any of the animals. Once a human touched them, the parents would reject them and sometimes abandon them. It was best just to let them be, for to have the human smell surely meant death for some.

Grandfather had also taught him that all things that have life will someday die. The trees and rocks, he said, were included in that life. He said water was sacred. It healed. He told him the story of how the Creator made the world and everything in it and became part of it. Kikto always thought of water as the blood of the great Grandfather.

Of the rocks, Grandfather said four kinds were considered to have sacred powers. The colors of the rocks are a deep brown, red, whitish and black. He told Kikto where each kind could be found and how to use them properly. Grandfather had told him to be observant in his travels and to be mindful of wind or *kxate*, to speak to him often. All this Kikto thought about as he lay resting. He soon fell asleep.

He had a dream. A cloud hovered over the teepee hole, and a voice called his name. As he looked up he was atop the cloud, and it raced across the prairies. The path he had traveled he could see. Soon he was above his camp in the mountains. The cloud hovered there as he looked down.

All the teepees were as when he had left. His grandparents now stood outside their teepee with his parents near them. He saw that they were happily going about their daily activities. He even saw his childhood friend. He was making a shield. This was all good to see. The voice that called his name now spoke: "Wanyanka yo!" (Observe!) which jolted Kikto awake far from his mountain home. It was still daylight and the dream seemed very real to him.

He decided to go in search of his herd. First, he walked down to the river. He found a crossing and went to the other side of the river and up along the draws which the herd liked best.

An old teepee trail led away from the crossing toward the hillside. He wished he had asked the names of the draws; most draws were named, and there were two or three just in that area. He chose the one that had a small stream running into the river. He followed the stream up the draw until he came to the top of the hill, where he could see for miles.

He looked all around. The land stretched out on the horizon. He was awed by the circle that surrounded them. It was always like that, except in the mountains where one could only see the eastern horizon. He stood in reverence to creation, feeling the sensation as birds chirped and gray squirrels clicked somewhere. Truly it was a gorgeous afternoon.

He whistled as he sat down on a boulder sticking out of the ground. He had heard of the snakes and spiders of the prairies. A question the medicine men often ask children came as a riddle. 'I am small with many legs, but I can kill you; what am I? *"Machik'ala na hu ma-ota, eyash chikte owakihi yelo; mataku hwo?"* The reply must be quick and correct. If one was asked the question and did not answer quickly enough, he or she was told to be quick with their thoughts. His or her life might depend on the ability to think quickly. Along with these thoughts, *Be knowledgeable and observant. Haven't the unci and Txunkashila told stories? Are you hearing what they have to say?* Grandfather had forewarned him of snakes and spiders that could kill him, and he was careful.

He had looked all around the two draws for his herd but seen nothing. He heard an animal blowing through his nostrils before he saw it. He turned toward the sound and found himself looking toward a grove of cedar trees. He saw nothing but heard the sound again. There must be another draw on that side, he thought as he walked in that direction. There was a draw! It had looked flat, but upon reaching the place where the sound had come from, he found he was standing on a ridge. His herd was grazing down in the valley.

He stood looking all around; he saw the tops of buttes, knolls, and the sharp-pointed buttes called *paha pestola*. The flat-topped buttes called paha usually were named after something or an event, such as Kangxi Paha or Crow Butte. It was a place where the birds loved to nest.

He counted his herd and noticed a new doe with his herd. She was of a different color and taller than the others. He looked at the leader and back at the new doe. Where had he found her? Where was her fawn? She must belong to another herd, a wild herd, nearby somewhere.

The sun was lowering on the horizon, painting the sky with beautiful colors. He reflected, *The Creator has made life beautiful for us. Each day when we see such wonders, it is He who has painted the sky, it is He who caps the mountains with ice and snow, it is He who colors the earth with such striking hues.*

As he walked back toward the camp, he could hear flutes, one was already singing a love song. The lyrics spoke of love from a distant past, the kind of love that does not die, but lives on through time. Without realizing it, he had stopped to listen. The song ended as another began somewhere across the hilltop.

He walked on, aware that he had to cross the river at the darkest time when day meets night. The water was perfect for swimming. He decided to swim. As he prepared to swim, he heard voices downstream. Others were swimming, and he decided to join them.

There were four or five swimmers. It was now past the darkest time of day—*xta-oiyokpaze*, it was called—and he could make out shadows. They were playing a water catch game. He often saw the game being played but had never joined the fun. He sat beside the river watching for a while, then went swimming.

He heard more voices downstream, those of young women with their chaperones who were swimming together. The moon had risen, and the water was beginning to cool down. He went to get his belongings, his breechcloth, and his moccasins.

Back at camp, fires were burning in front of teepees. The main fire where storytelling or *ohunkankan* took place was a glowing amber. A man came singing along the teepees. Some children followed dancing. Others joined in until many people came to the center of the camp, called *chokata*, where they sang and continued dancing. Kikto knew that there would not be any storytelling that night. He would wait, he was patient.

The eyapaha followed Kikto to the teepee where he and Iyeshni were staying. He sat down and asked Kikto about his camp. Kikto told him that his camp was in the mountains and storytelling was the main event in the evenings. The eyapaha agreed that indeed storytelling was an important event.

Here at this camp, *ohunkankan* was reserved for certain nights. Grandmothers told nighttime stories in each teepee at bedtime, the eyapaha said. He added that as long as he could remember, it had been so in his camp. On special days like today, when the sunset was as beautiful as it had been, people danced. Other nights, when the sky was clear and the stars were bright, it was time for *ohunkankan*, he said.

The eyapaha took the opportunity to tell Kikto about their camp. They were planters and traders, he said. When crops were ready they took them to the trading towns. They had two favorite places. One was called Stone Village or *Iyan Otxunwahe*, and the other was farther to the southwest, a town called Waterfalls Village or *Mini Xaxa Otxunwahe*. It was called that for the many waterfalls and streams that descended from the hills and bluffs. The place was thought of as a sacred place, the eyapaha said.

The one nearest to them, *Iyan Otxunwahe*, was where they would be traveling to in a few days. There were villages along this river, mud huts, earth lodges, and teepees. Many people dwelled there and spoke different languages. It would be the first time Kikto would meet people from many different tribes. Other tribes people lived different from Kikto's people.

They were not hunters like the Prairie Dwellers or *Thitxunwan*, with whom they traded for buffalo meat and hides. The hunters, he said, wanted the planted crops, especially dried corn or *washtunkala*. They also wanted corn or *wagmiza*. There were many different kinds of vegetables. At these trading places beautifully designed animal hides were made and traded. Fresh meat and hides were in demand. Many people traveled to this place to trade informed the eyapaha.

There were shield makers, bow and arrow makers, and lance makers. Some of these items took up to three, maybe four years to make, depending on the kind of wood. In his village they had a shield maker, he said.

Pottery makers, who shaped dishes and containers of various kinds and sizes, also traded their goods. The hide tanners made storage boxes, pipe bags, and other such containers. Most women knew how to make these items, but the fun was in the trade, he said.

For all these items and more, they traded their squash, turnip braids, onions, corn, wild garlic, and other vegetables. In addition, his relatives made quilled moccasins, vests, dresses, and other clothing. Some of the young men in his camp hunted and traded the hooves of the deer and claws of various kinds.

At the time of trading, the eyapaha continued, there were other activities going on such as racing. Shooting the arrow to the sky, target shooting and the girls had a marble contest, hand games, and much more.

After the trading was over, they would travel to their winter camps in the Xe Sapa. They would leave some of their summer belongings at their summer camps and take their winter supplies to their winter camps. *Caves or Washun*, the eyapaha said, were used to store their goods. Some people actually lived in the caves. Once they arrived at their winter camp, he continued, *ohunkankan* took place nightly there. There they would meet other relatives who had gone to different summer camps. At the time when they returned, they would find some of the children had grown, or there would be new family members.

"The children," he said, "need to hear about the way they are to live, how to treat others, and how to take care of the land upon which they walk as two-legged beings; they need to know which four-leggeds to eat and which to fear. Also the winged ones and the creatures of the waters all need to have a certain place; these things we teach our children at the winter camps.

"In addition," he continued, "children need to hear about creation, how the world, the sun, the moon, and the stars all came to be. Where did water come from? What about fire? All these things children must know."

At this point, the eyapaha asked, by request of the people of the village, that Kikto accompany them to the trade town. He told Kikto they knew about his herd of antelope and believed that he might be able to trade some there at Iyan Otxunwahe. Many people would want to trade for the animals, as their hides were useful and soft for making children's clothes.

Kikto said he hoped that his herd would grow in numbers. Eyapaha countered by pointing out that the meat of the antelope was good to eat. It had a unique flavor, as they ate sage. He went on to say that the people had offered to take Kikto's trade goods to their winter camp; his mountain village was less than a moon away from them.

In the way of the people, he knew that he had a choice. It would not be a burden for them to carry his belongings to the Black Mountains or Xe Sapa with them. They already knew that Kikto and Iyeshni would not be traveling back with them. This made him realize that they knew his purpose. It was close to the turn of the century.

The eyapaha told him that in two nights there would be storytelling. It would be the women, he said, who would talk about the stars that helped them prepare their gardens. They would tell the name of each moon during the time of raising their crops. Kikto sat gazing at the stars as the eyapaha spoke. This was an event that was done before going to the trade towns. The eyapaha continued, saying that voices carried far into space, traveling upward without stopping; this, he said, was considered sacred. By telling their stories, the women would pass on the tradition to future planters, and by sending their voices, they would convey to the Creator how much the women appreciated the growth of their crops.

Another dawn had arrived, and after the morning song the eyapaha had awakened the village. Some of the people stood outside their teepees as he sang the morning song, men, women, and children alike.

Some of the women raised both hands in the direction of the rising sun as they sang along with the eyapaha.

The feeling of being one with creation washed over Kikto. His feet seemed to sink deep into the earth while his upper body rose high into the sky. He could not only see all around him but also felt himself opening, almost like a flower blooming and feeling a deep union with all. It lasted a short time, but it seemed like ages. In this instant he sensed where his herd was and felt a connection with their leader. He felt that the leader also sensed this.

The sun had risen. The eyapaha announced that there would be *ohunkankan* that night. Everyone tended to their morning chores. There was not a soul who was not moving. The children agreed to be awake that night, as it was a special night of storytelling, and they all wanted to hear these special stories by the women.

A feast was announced. Kikto wondered about this as he had not seen any fresh meat yesterday. He wondered what kind of feast was held without fresh meat. When the sun was high overhead, he noticed some of the women carrying stones to the east part of the camp. They lined the inside of shallow pits with these stones, lining the bottoms with the flattest ones and the sides with more rounded ones.

Then they built fires in each of the pits. The women were talking and laughing as they worked. Some men had come to help, and Kikto joined them. He was curious about how the firepits were built and lined. He also wondered if the men in this village did the cooking for a feast, as it was done in his village. He was prepared to help, although he did not know exactly what he should do.

The women prepared the vegetables to be roasted while the men prepared the cooking items to be used for that purpose. The eyapaha had returned from somewhere and explained to Kikto that the men cooked at the feasts. He asked if it was the same at his village. Kikto replied that it was.

Now as he watched, women husked corn, removing only the hair and some of the inside layers. Then they tied the outer husks back into place. These ears they placed around the inner edge of the layered stones. Next they placed quartered squash over the outer edge. The seeds were laid in the sun to dry.

He noticed some of the children washing some of the seeds. He wondered if they roasted them the way he had done when he was very young. When they turned brown, they were crunchy and tasty. He noticed the women were now holding dried fat on sticks over the squash, which melted right onto the tops of the squash. Turnips and onions were prepared for the soup.

Grandmothers took grandchildren with them to the marshy area of the river to gather a tuber called *blo* or potato, also for the stew. Soon the air filled with the aroma of cooking foods, and Kikto's stomach growled. He kept busy, putting more wood in the firepits and pitching in with the men's other chores.

A larger fire pit was started as in Kikto's vision, when he traveled on a cloud to his village. Again he wondered about meat. The familiar buffalo stomach pouch called *chegxa* was now hung over the fire on a tripod made of willow trees. Into this they put the prepared vegetables to cook. Kikto was thinking about offering one of his lean makhicima when he heard the trills of the women. It meant either hunters or warriors returning. He looked in the direction of the trilling and saw some young men coming down the hill with meat.

After setting down the buffalo meat, they continued on down to the river to bathe. They had been gone for two days, the eyapaha said. The men now began cutting the meat into smaller pieces to roast. The scent of roasting meat now blended with the other enticing aromas. Not a single human or animal stomach remained quiet as they anticipated the feast.

Shortly the hunters returned from the river. They told of their hunt. They had gotten the buffalo about a day and a half walk from camp. Appropriately, they left some of the fat and other parts for the wolves or *shungmanitu*. They wrapped the rest of the meat in the hides for the dog drags. They carried what they could. Last night, they said, they rested in a wooded area where they were able to hang the meat overnight so the blood could drain.

Now back at camp, the men worked on removing the brains; the tongue had been previously removed. At this point two of the hunters came to take the heads to an ant pile up along the ridge so the ants could eat. This would also finish cleaning the skulls; the ants, with the help of other small animals, would remove the rest of the hide ears and other parts that were still on the heads. This was another way for the people to share their food. When winter had come and gone and summer was back, the skulls would be clean—if bigger animals did not carry them away, as they sometimes did.

Kikto wondered about mushrooms or *channakpa*. In this village he had not seen any. Most people ate them fresh, but it had not rained for a few days. The food was now almost cooked. He helped roast the meat to put into the soup.

People were now gathered at the center of the village. Kikto noticed that the eating utensils were made of wood, ceramic, and rawhide shaped into bowls with willow sticks, the kind used to make the strong spears. He wanted one of those for his grandfather. He also noticed that they had short sticks sharpened at the tips for spearing their meat.

The eyapaha announced that the meal was to be served soon; *"Hiyu po, wota po!"* he yelled in all directions. More people began to gather at the center. Kikto noticed that the children sat first in the center, where the leader and the men usually sit. The elderly were directly behind them, with the women and men at the outer edge. The children and elderly were served first. The hunters and other young men now gathered the eating utensils of the children and elderly and took them to the fire pits where the servers tended to them. Each person had their own eating utilities.

The serving was meticulous. The children and elderly each had something from each food cooked in the fire pits. After the children and elderly were served, all others stood and formed lines at each of the fire pits to serve themselves. Soon the eyapaha began sending his voice to the four corners of the universe to ask for blessings for the food, to bring good health to those who ate the food and good feelings for all, "… for when the two-legged are happy so are the ones in the other world." He ended with *"Mitakuye Owas'in"*; all in unison replied, *"Hau, hau, tosh, washté,"* and even the children chorused their thanksgiving.

Iyeshni sat with his relatives and reserved a spot for Kikto, who had been helping with the serving. Iyeshni's relatives treated him as an honored guest. Honored guests were not allowed to serve. Kikto was just the kind of person who did what his heart desired, it was his nature.

"There is no one above another in our way of life," grandfather had told him many times. "There is a time and place and a purpose for each person. Sometimes you are honored; sometimes you honor others. It is meant to be so. Observe what it is that you are being honored for at that time that is your purpose. In time you will find your real life purpose." He added, "In your life you have a very special duty to fulfill. Do it in honor of the people, never expect to be honored, that is not your way. Your way, your purpose is to fulfill a prophecy that comes directly from the Creator; keep that always in your mind and your heart." Said grandfather.

He smiled at Iyeshni, who returned the smile, rubbing his stomach. By the time the feast was done, the sun was at the highest point in the sky. Some people had gone back to their teepees, carrying leftovers or *watxeca* to eat later. Today the wasna was excellent. Kikto took some fresh wasna to put in his bag.

Chapter 6

Wakinyan Thunderbeing

The entire camp was now quiet. Suddenly an older woman began yelling, "Wakinyan aku! Wakinyan aku!" (The thunder being is returning, the thunder being is returning!) She ran to her teepee and went inside, closing the flaps and tying down the bottom. The camp was now bustling with people briskly closing their teepee flaps. Each teepee was dug out all around the base so water would not flow inside.

A little boy called Chaské came running to help his grandmother. He was the firstborn boy or the firstborn son, which was why he was called Chaské. His real name was not used; instead he was called by different names. Some called him Ishnala which means Alone or the only child.

Kikto had heard a low rumbling to the southwest, yet he saw no clouds. How did that woman know that it was going to rain? He saw birds flying in disarray between the river and the camp. Other birds joined them. Then he noticed the black cloud rolling slowly across the southwest horizon. It quickly darkened like evening, and he saw streaks of lightning and loud thunder resonating across the black cloud.

He was thinking about the thunder being. Wakinyan was feared, as she was the main helper between the Creator and common man or *ikce wichasha*. When the two-leggeds were not obedient to the values given by the Creator, He would send her to punish them. She was given the power to make wind, water, ice, and fire. The Creator gave her these powers when her husband went hunting and never returned.

Her constant state of emotion is anger. When she opens her eyes, flashes of light burst from them. She often bellows for her husband; other times she opens her wings and her little ones all clap their hands at the same time so their father would hear them and come home. She returns in early spring and leaves in the fall to a cave inside the Black Hills. Year after year she and her young ones look for her husband. People know when she is in search of her husband and when the Creator has sent her by the manner of her appearance. This was the story his grandfather told him.

As Kikto stood looking upward, suddenly life around him seemed to become silent, even the air seemed to stop—then, *crack!* Raindrops exploded from the sky. The delighted children watched the rain until they were called into the teepees.

Kikto had never experienced such a storm. Rain gushed, thunder bellowed and light flashed everywhere! It seemed Wakinyan was in search of her husband as she hovered for a while and then continued her wandering. After she had passed, the sun came out shining brightly. Water flowed everywhere; children came out and waded and splashed. *That was a fast storm* was the general comment.

Many people gazed at the eastern horizon where a bright rainbow had formed. Dark clouds slowly drifted eastward beyond the rainbow. The air smelled bitingly fresh. Butterflies and children darted here and there as the birds seemed to sing an after-the-rain song. Earth was restored once again.

The camp prepared for storytelling to take place that night. After the ground had dried, the main fire pit was rekindled. It blazed for a while, dying down to embers as people gathered for story time. The sun had set with its usual flaming display. What a beautiful sight to Kikto's eyes! Now the sky was clear, and the stars twinkled brightly. It was a good night for storytelling.

Cedar branches that had been previously gathered and dried were now set alight and carried around the circle of people. Families sat together for this occasion. The burning of the cedar continued until its fragrance was everywhere. Soon the oldest woman in the camp arrived at the center. She began her story by pointing to a star above them. This star, she said, belongs to the women.

She continued, "The women of the past watched for the appearance of this bright star to know when to begin planting. Tonight," she said as she sprinkled sweet grass over the embers producing a pleasant smell in the air, "it is higher in the sky than when it first appeared in the eastern horizon. We use this star to tell us when we will plant our crop." She finished.

Another woman stood and said, "Chinshka," pointing to the seven stars making up that constellation. "We watch to know if we will have rain or not. If it tilts forward, we will get rain; if not, then it will be dry. We are diligent once we begin our gardens. The stars in the sky change positions, traveling with us, telling us of what is to come." She added a little more of the sweet grass to the glowing embers.

A woman who was still able to conceive stood next. "We count the phases of the moon to help us cultivate our gardens. We name each moon for the fruits that ripen. We await the moon we call *wasutxun* so that we may harvest our crop and prepare for trading." She continued, "We also count the phases of the moon to know which moon we will conceive. We care for our crops and our infants with the same guiding hands."

She sat down, as another woman stood and pointed to two stars just southeast of the zenith. "At the beginning of the summer when our crops are still young, we gaze at the stars in the nighttime. We search for those two stars so that we may know when exactly to dig our tinpsila. We know by the position of the stars that the flower on the tinpsila plant will soon bud, and then we may dig in preparation for the new winter." She also added cedar to the fire pit, adding to the pleasant scent.

Kikto listened as more women told their stories. He had not known so many stories related to the planting of the crops, nor did he know how important the moon phases were. He had even more thoughts to ponder about the night sky.

Now another woman stood. She was known to be the bear healer in the village. She pointed to a group of stars toward the northeast shaped like a dome. This group of stars, she said, was called Matxo Teepeela. It appeared at a certain place in the sky when it was time to pick certain berries and to keep the sacredness of the pits of these berries.

"*Kxanta shasha* is the ripening of the plums," she said. "The seeds are sacred *wakxan*. It must be twin girls who teach their sons how to use the sacred seeds to keep track of their history. Each must put the seeds in a wooden bowl and take her son up to the top of a hill, where she must show him the star that will help him keep in his memory the events."

This was not the same as keeping track of events on a buffalo robe, she said. This was a way to keep track of the ordinary things that people did in everyday life. "Remember," she said, "it must be the son of a twin girl who is taught this way." She threw some dried plum leaves in the fire pit.

It was late, and the stars seemed to shine brighter and twinkle in countless colors. Still, the storytelling went on. Kikto noticed how quiet it was during this time; everyone listened entranced, and no one interrupted. He knew from his own village that if there were any questions, they were to be saved for Grandmother or Grandfather at a later time.

For four nights such storytelling took place. The stories were about not only the stars but places such as caves in the Black Mountains, the rivers, lakes, and boulders, the ancestors, and much more. There were stories of animals, people, birds, and other events; both men and women told stories, some of them humorous. Kikto was filled with all these stories. Someday, he thought, a grandchild would hear about this time in his life.

Early in the morning of the fifth day, many from camp were ready for travel. Some of the children and older people, too young or too old to travel to the trade village, would stay here at this camp.

Kikto did not realize that he was ready to move on. He felt he had been in one place too long. He was use to moving about with his herd for days at a time, seeing no other human beings.

Some women took down the lodge where he and Iyeshni were living. They prepared it for travel, tying the packed teepee to one of the travel dogs. They would care for it until they got to the trading town.

After the morning song, as soon as the packing was done, everyone was ready to travel. The eyapaha led the people in single file, walking along an old travel path. It reached the base of a slope and led them zigzagging upward toward the ridge. When they reached the top they stopped and looked back to see where they had come from. The village had a few teepees standing, and thin smoke spiraled upward from the fire pits.

At this point the eyapaha sang a travel song, sending his voice in different directions as others joined him. One of the men, who was standing a little away from the village watching, now heard the song and joined he singing. He recalled his younger days when travel was easy. Now he watched as the travelers disappeared beyond the ridge.

The travelers continued walking even as they sang the wordless song. The eyapaha's family led the group, with the leader and his family following. Later just the women and children would walk on the drag trail, and the men would walk on the footpaths alongside. As Kikto looked at the group, he could not tell which women were the storytellers of the first night. He did know that they were part of the group now traveling to the trade town.

Some of the women carried babies on cradle boards strapped to their backs. Young boys and girls carried younger siblings on their backs on a buffalo hide backpack made just for them. This helped to keep their weights evenly balanced. Soon, however, they would be put in carriers for the dogs that were not pulling teepees.

Some of the bigger dogs pulled these willow hut carriers with smaller children and their pets. Other dogs pulled the trade goods. The older boys and girls walked alongside the convoy. At times the boys would stray off and disappear behind the hills, but they always returned and stayed nearby.

The scouts were somewhere far ahead and to each side and behind as well. The eyapaha told Kikto they always traveled like this for at least four or five days before they reached Iyan Otxunwahe.

Kikto spotted his herd on the ridge across the river. He knew he could count on his lead antelope to follow; the herd was accustomed to moving camps. He was amazed at how the lead had always able to stay with the people, even when he was younger. He would not lose sight of Kikto.

Soon the travelers arrived at a point of a ridge or *ipxa* that led down to the river they had been traveling above. An old trail led down all the way to the riverbanks and across. People had traveled this way perhaps for centuries.

At the foot of this ridge when everyone had safely descended, the eyapaha announced that they would rest and eat here, as the sun was now in the middle of the sky. There was no need to remind people to eat lightly. They were aware of protocol.

They ate and rested while children and dogs played in the water. One of them spotted a turtle or *kheya*. Smaller children wanted to ride it, as their older siblings did; however, they were too young and too slow in case the turtle tried to bite.

The eyapaha told Kikto that this crossing was called Bobcat Crossing or *Igmuglezela Iyuwegxe* . It was well known that the bobcats lived in the draws near here. This alerted Kikto to think of his herd; bobcats were known to kill deer if there were enough of them to attack and they were hungry. He motioned to Iyeshni that he was going across the river to check his herd and stay near them.

Kikto started away from camp, his dog following. The eyapaha told Kikto that there were two scouts on each side of the river. One had returned and told him that Kikto's herd was safe. He also said that the bobcats had been moving toward the west in the last two days.

Kikto said all this was good; however, he wanted to count his herd. He told the eyapaha that he would meet them farther down the river. The eyapaha told him that there was one steep hillside where they would have to climb higher just to go back down again; he said this is where they would camp. He said there were two creeks that flowed into the larger river. One of the creeks was called Cherry Creek or *Chanpxa Wakpa*, and Plum Creek or *Kxanta Wakpa*. They were on the opposite sides of the river. Chanpxa Wakpa flowed from a northerly direction, while Kxanta Wakpa flowed from the south.

He also told Kikto that the sacred hot springs were in the area on the side of where *Chanpxa Wakpa* lies. They would bathe in the night, and the women and children would bathe in the morning.

Kikto set out to find his herd. High atop the ridge he gave a low whistle and waited. Nothing, no reply. Where was the usual snort of his leader? He whistled again as he moved farther along the ridge. He saw people moving below as he walked along the rim. He had walked for some time when he gave the low whistle again. This time he heard a reply, the short snort. It was a game between them when they were younger, now it worked for them.

He walked in the direction of the snort and soon found the herd. They were in a valley near a spring. He counted them, noticing the larger female was still with the herd. It seemed as if she were here to stay. He wondered what her offspring would look like.

He was happy that he had found them as he heard a low growl later in the evening. He sat up and looked around. He knew that if the cats were hungry enough, they would attack this herd. They were lying in a close group not far from him. This kept them safe, as other animals, including bobcats, did not like the scent of humans. The leader was standing as if on guard close to the mothers and their young.

Kikto now patrolled the area and settled above the herd. His dog was close at his heels. If needed, the dog was a ferocious fighter. Kikto had been listening but heard nothing more. He fixed his bed and slept lightly. He was awakened by another sound. The eyapaha was singing the sunrise song, and it echoed in the draws, resonating all around them. He knew that they had camped somewhere nearby.

Kikto whistled for the leader who approached. He spoke to him in human language to stay near the people. The leader seemed to understand. In fact the whole herd seemed to understand. The usually shy young ones had approached him as well, this was the closest they had ever come.

He did his morning rituals with the exception of the song, as he heard the eyapaha and others singing. He walked slowly down a deer trail leading toward the river. The area was wrapped in a blue haze, through which he could see trees along the opposite hills and more draws and trails. There was a smell of burning wood and meat cooking over the fires. He continued down the trail as the deer followed.

He reached camp as they prepared to travel. They had packed their belongings. They had not set up teepees but instead built willow huts. The women and children had returned from bathing in the sacred water. Even though the men had bathed the night before, Kikto decided he would bathe before continuing on the journey.

Now the entire group was walking south along the creek called Kxanta Wakpa. The trail ran along the creek on both sides as trails usually did. At some point one of the trails would lead away from the creek. They traveled on the east side of the creek and continued until the sun was high in the sky.

One of the scouts returned and said they had found a good spot to camp for the night, farther up the creek. After they had rested and refreshed themselves, the group continued on along the creek.

Near sunset one of the scouts returned to tell them they were near the camping spot. After traveling a bit further, the group arrived at the designated campsite. Here they took the children out of the carriers and unpacked the dogs. Both the children and dogs were excited! They all scampered off toward the clear-flowing creek.

Meanwhile the adults found the willow groves and made their overnight shelters. The tops of the willows were pulled together to form small huts called *thiyuktan*. The grass beneath was already flattened, as people had traveled through here recently, perhaps less than a moon ago. The shelters they made would keep them dry from the early morning rains.

The next morning after their rituals, the group ate a light meal and traveled on. Soon they came to a fork in the creek, one stream led toward the west while the other between south and east. Having traveled this route for many summers, the eyapaha led them eastward. They followed the shallow creek for nearly the whole day, and finally the path led away from the creek, upward toward the flats.

Kikto had rejoined them the day before now observed the area. There were groves of trees that he was certain concealed small water holes. He had seen many of these on his journey from the mountains. He continued to gaze all around, seeing buttes that seemed to be close but he knew were far away. He knew the land was deceiving. They would travel under the sun for a long time before they would even come near one of the buttes, if that was their goal.

Two days later they camped near a spring. A small stream flowed away from the spring. There were berry bushes everywhere, along with cedar, pine, and nut trees. A tall tree whose bark was white stood higher than the others, and wrapped around the branches of this tree were grape vines.

Kikto was told to look carefully in the water for a thin white substance. If the spring showed signs of this substance then, it was bitter water or *skuya* and not drinkable.

There was a story told for generations. When a lake dried up, out in the center was a thick white substance. This substance was hard to get, as the center was soft mud, and one could easily sink in and never be seen again. This substance was called salt or mini skuya. It was said that only the smallest of the young men were able to walk to the center to get it.

Kikto never had to worry about finding water, as his herd led him to some of the sweetest waters he had ever tasted, in the springs closer to his mountain home. His mountain home was far away; in fact, looking westward, he could no longer see the Xe Sapa in the horizon. Here in this place the air was different. It felt moist to the body, not only that there was a fragrance in the air that was unfamiliar, but pleasant.

They continued to travel without delay. Travel was good. Now it seemed the women and children were walking faster than usual. Even the dogs seemed excited. The travelers continued their brisk pace.

Soon they came to the top of another hill. As they reached the top of this hill, Kikto noticed that he was looking back each time they reached the top of a hill. He wondered about this as they continued. *Our ancestors*, he thought, *traveled these same paths that we are now walking. Did they look back?—and if they did, did they see what I see?* ,

As he looked forward on the trail they were now following, a bluish hazy fog materialized across the entire horizon. It looked as if the Milky Way or Wanagxi Txachanku had fallen upon the earth under the sun! The blue haze began near the southern horizon and flowed far off to the north. He was not aware that he was holding his breath until he exhaled. He had experienced similar fog in the mountains, but out here, where there were no trees, it was breathtaking. In the mountains it was caused by the moisture of a large lake and was called Makxa Txa-oniye. He would ask the eyapaha later what it was called here.

Eyapaha announced that they would soon arrive at Iyan Otxunwahe or Stone Village. As they neared the village, which was not in view, Kikto could see other travelers moving toward the same destination. He wondered if he would know any of them. He could not feel the same anticipation or excitement as the others. He had not experienced this before.

They continued crossing deep ravines, dry streambeds of the kind formed by heavy rains. They would get to a hilltop only to head downward again. It was extremely tiring for many of the women and children; however, that did not lessen their excitement. Soon they arrived at a much larger creek. Here they rested in the shade of some trees. The eyapaha told the people to eat a little something, but no one seemed to be hungry. Children and dogs played along the creek. They would find a shallow crossing.

Near where they stopped was a beaver dam. The young beavers came out of their dens to peer at the noise outside. The children and dogs saw the pair of dark eyes as a small beaver appeared between the logs, his home. The children now sat quiet as they watched what the newcomer would do. Even the dogs seemed to be waiting. He climbed the log where he could look toward where the larger group sat talking and laughing. One of the children sneezed, and the young beaver darted into his den.

Excited children returned to their families to tell them of seeing the young beaver, the dogs jumping excitedly as if to confirm their sighting. It was time to move on. Everyone crossed the creek where the older boys had found a path. They crested the hill where Kikto saw the river and the villages at the same time. He could see across the river where the rocks and waterfalls cascaded toward the bottom, and at the bottom there were more rocks.

People were everywhere! He could see smoke rising from the centers of the earth lodges or *thigmigma* and in front of the teepee camps. The river curved sharply toward the east, and a deep river flowed in from the west. He looked toward the fork in the river or okhizhata and saw, along the smaller river, more teepee camps and a few more earth lodges. Kikto wanted badly to go inside one of the earth lodges. It was the first time he had seen the lodges.

To the north were more earth lodges. People were arriving in groups from all directions, even across the river. A trail led downward from across the wide river, and at the bottom of this slope was a crossing. The crossing had many bull boats or *wata*. The men who owned these helped others cross the river to the west bank.

Further north on the west bank was the trade center or village. Already there were many campers, who settled in groups as they arrived. The eyapaha went to a campsite with his weary but excited travelers. He told Kikto that it was the same place they had always camped. For many winters his ancestors came here to trade and camped in the same place.

The women quickly set up camp. The men had to raise the teepee poles like they always did. They did this after the women stretched the buffalo hides over the poles. Once the teepees were raised, the men went about doing other chores. The women unpacked everything, separating trade goods from their personal belongings.

So many people in one place! The eyapaha said different nations met here to trade. They used words from each other's languages to convey the items for trade. In addition, they used gestures to communicate. The eyapaha often knew languages other than their own. Some knew up to three or four. Some of the women who lived in this town intermarried and could speak the language of their husbands. Their children likewise knew more than one language.

The eyapaha found some young men around the age of Kikto and Iyeshni and asked them to take the pair on a tour. They agreed. Soon they went on a tour; they walked toward the okhizhata and the camps there. Kikto would just have to wait to see the inside of an earth lodge. Soon they came to the river, where one of the guides suggested they tour on a wata. Neither Kikto nor Iyeshni had ever been on this sort of boat and decided they should wait until later. This was the first trading trip that Iyeshni had participated.

All along the river were people swimming or sunning and others sleeping. Weary travelers rested along the river, while others like Kikto and Iyeshni went on tours. Others were crossing the river to see family across the river.

A man who had taken a woman and her two children across the river was returning alone. It looked as if he was walking on an invisible road upon the waters! As he neared, he yelled, "Hau!" using the traditional male greeting as he climbed out of his boat onto the shore. He asked Kikto and Iyeshni to which camp they belonged.

The boatman studied the pair recognizing that neither one belonged to any of the recent arrivals. Older people recognized people from their style of dress. Both these young men were dressed differently, even from each other. The boatman was surprised to hear 'Hoxwozhu' and realized that they were part of the Tetons or Thitxunwan. They lived along the Long River or Mini Hanska in the Plains and planted crops. They brought their harvest to trade. They continued to explain that Kikto belonged to one of the campfires of the mountains or Xe

Ska. This older man now studied the two young men intently, as it was the tradition.

As they finished explaining their roots, the boatman told Iyeshni his father's name. Then he gave Kikto a strange look and asked his name. "Kiktopawingxa," came the reply. He then asked for the name of Kikto's grandmother, again a proper question. "Khugyuhamaniwin," he replied. Silence. Since it was clear the boatman was thinking about grandparents, he offered his grandfather's name: "Watxoye" to which the boatman acknowledged realizing Kikto's mission.

Two young ladies appeared with their chaperones. The boatman knew them, as he had taken them across many times. It was considered disrespectful for the young men to converse with them. They both now turned in a direction away from them. The boatman announced his departure with one of the young ladies and her chaperone. The other with her chaperone now left, waving good-bye to her friend.

Trading, games and several activities for the young people went on each day. It was announced one evening that there would be storytelling by some of the most knowledgeable storytellers! Kikto keenly looked forward to the event. Young men who were participating made announcements, the way an Eyapaha would, announcing the trade goods from their camp.

The sunset and evening activities were occurring in various places. The storytellers would be at the center of the trading place. A fire pit was lit, flames rose high into the air, and the smell of wood burning permeated all around.

People began gathering at the center. This was the main trading place. Young men were practicing the art of being an eyapaha, which always drew a humorous response. People laughed as the young men made statements that an eyapaha would make, only in a joking manner, as was expected of them. One yelled, "Mitakuyepi! Anagxoptan po! Howakankan kte lo!" Laughter burst out all around in the circle. Others made similar statements, to similar response. Humor was one of the best teachers; everyone knew this.

Storytelling was long that night, and Kikto heard different versions of some of the same stories. The protocol was the same. Tonight it was the men who did the storytelling. The stories were of hunting places that Kikto had not heard of, along with boulders and crossings, including how some had received their names. One told his winter count story which was quite young compared to others who had older ones.

One of the final storytellers was a history keeper of the Sacred Plum Seeds. It was the first time Kikto had heard one of these. It was about the history of trading center of Stone Village. There were the usual sounds of agreement, "Hau, han, tosh, hechetu welo!" all around.

When Kikto returned to their teepee, Iyeshni was already sleeping. Kikto sat close to the fire pit and marked the end of another day on one of the sticks used for counting days. It was how those who kept the winter counts kept track of days. He had been counting the days and nights. He used red for the day and blue for the night.

All too soon, it seemed, the eyapaha came and announced their departure. He announced that the people had traded all their goods and were now ready to return to their summer camp. They also wanted to get a good start toward their winter camp in the Xe Sapa. Having announced their intentions, he retired for the night. Moving camp announcements were made at night so people could be properly rested and ready for travel the next day.

Kikto and Iyeshni walked with them for a day and spent the night with them. Kikto had traded some of his herd. A young boy wanted a female for a pet. It was traded for maple syrup or *chanhanpi* that his grandmother wanted, along with some baskets and other goods for his mother and one of her sisters. He kept the items to just a few, as he did not want to burden those who would carry them.

Early the next morning they sang the sunrise song together. The people left toward where the sun goes down, while Iyeshni and Kikto, along with his herd, went back to Iyan Otxunwahe. It took most of the day. The trip back was quicker than when they traveled in a group.

At the top of the hill they stopped and looked at the now-familiar place. There were a few traders left. Some people were leaving, returning along the trails on which they had arrived. A group sang as departed singing a beautiful travel song that had words in it. Most travel songs were wordless.

Upon arriving at their teepee, they found that a female cousin had made them wasna and left some dried fat. Men utilized dried fat for painting. Kikto had a need for dried fat to continue to paint on the wolf hide that would be sent with runners to the mountains. The pictures would later be transferred to buffalo hide so they would last longer.

Kikto recalled how his grandfather taught him how to paint using the fine powder colors mixed with the fat and a little water. His first painting was on a rabbit hide, and his grandmother had hung it proudly in front of her teepee and invited some of her relatives to come and eat so she might present the hide painting. Now, in a town far away from the mountains, he could hear his grandfather's words: "When one has a purpose in life, one should not worry about anything. For those who keep their purpose in mind, everything will fall into place for them."

Today he marveled at his grandfather's wisdom. Everything was happening as if it were planned. He and Iyeshni would spend the winter in this village.

Now they returned to find their teepee was the only one standing alone in a meadow, away from the earth lodges and the other teepees and far from the river. But not for long!

The eyapaha from one of the teepee camps came by and asked how long they planned on staying here in town. They told him through the winter. The eyapaha then invited them to camp in his people's teepee camp, telling them the winters here could be harsh. He also said they would have to prepare for winter soon.

The eyapaha gestured as he spoke so Iyeshni would know what was going on as well. He also told them that some women would come and take down the teepee and raise it again in its new location. They just had to take their belongings and pick a spot.

They each tied their belonging to their pack dogs. The eager dogs appeared ready to travel far not knowing they had only a short distant to travel, it made both young men laugh. The dogs had such a look of dignity as they set off with their packs that the young men appreciated them even more.

The eyapaha had gone ahead to get the women and to wait for the young men to come choose a spot. Along the way, they met several women who were coming to take their teepee down. They did not speak, as it was considered disrespectful to speak to women who were alone. The exception was if they were relatives.

Upon reaching camp, they found the eyapaha waiting near some trees. The dogs looked at them questioningly as they unpacked them. They had gone such a short distance!

Soon the women arrived with the teepee and teepee poles. They raised the teepee in a very short time. It was placed where someone had left that day. The fire pit was already dug, and the women lined it with flat stones. The teepee was set up and the two went inside to choose a spot for themselves each avoiding the women's side. Kikto thought of his grandmother as he looked toward the women's side of the teepee. At that moment Kikto felt a deep connection to his grandparents' teepee back in the mountains. It felt good. He knew his grandparents prayed for him often.

Having finished they went back outside to help the other men carry the heavy hardwood from one of the places where the women got their firewood. This was done in preparation for winter fuel.

The next morning they decided to go explore across the river. They had not explored there yet, being busy with trading and games. Now they approached the man with the boat to ferry them across. When they reached the other side, they walked up a well-traveled path leading to some natural hot springs, the sacred bathing place. There they found women, children, and young women with their chaperones.

Nearby they noticed a young man around their age washing a wound. Kikto asked how he got the wound. He told them his camp had been attacked by some wandering group, and the defenders had killed most of them except for the one sitting there. He pointed to a young man sitting with guards around him.

This young man was referred to as a captured person or *wayaka* which meant he would be kept a prisoner until he learned the language and ways of the people. After his learning he would be set free to return to his own people.

Often when captives are set free they ask to return with their families to live amongst the people who they considered their enemy at one time. They did so because they liked this peaceful way of life.

Kikto and Iyeshni now walked up the hill where the rocks were larger, smooth, and colorful. The rocks surrounded the hillside. Beyond the rocks, in a ravine, was a waterfall or *minixaxa*. Kikto thought he would like to go there, but perhaps later. He was sure that courting would be taking place there. He wanted to hear some of the love songs played on the flute.

He wondered about the cave underneath the waterfall. Were there pictures on the cave walls, and who put them there? How long ago? He was curious. He loved the rainbow at the waterfalls. The air smelled fresh, and the mist coming from it was refreshing.

They met a young man who asked them many questions. He told Kikto that he looked very different from anyone he had ever seen, different from the rest of the people. He asked where he came from. Kikto said he was from Xe Ska or the White Mountains. The young man introduced himself as Looks Out or *Wakhita*.

Wakhita told Kikto and Iyeshni he would love to be their guide; he was born here and knew many interesting places to show them. They agreed. He also said he knew one of the keepers of the sacred fire who was able to speak three languages that were spoken right here in this area.

Kikto told him about Iyeshni and how they needed one who knew the sign language. Wakhita gestured as he talked to Kikto about how happy he was that they would let him show them around the area. They shook hands in agreement. Wakhita was now their official guide.

They began walking along the ridge leading toward the river. The islands or *wita* were occupied by many people. Wakhita told him that in the winter it was fun because they were able to walk on the ice to the islands to play games with their friends and relatives. Of these games he said he liked the ice games.

Wakhita told them two stories of how the place was named Iyan Otxunwahe. The first story involved some people who built their homes using the rocks, dirt, and a sand mixture. The second story, he said, made more sense. He told that because of the many stones in the area, one could see how that might be the source of the name, as they now walked on the stones to reach the riverbanks. Kikto now thought of his grandfather, who had told him always to listen to how places got named. Grandfather told him that there were almost always two stories, and both usually made sense.

The river seemed to be wider and bluer from where they were. Again Kikto recalled his grandfather's words about the color of water.

He said water had no color; it was the reflection of the sky that made it look blue. He had told Kikto to be observant of such things in the future.

By now they were at the banks of the river where more boats were available. They wanted to go across to the other side. They had not been up there before. Trails led upward from the river. There was a small village hidden behind the trees. It was the first time Kikto and Iyeshni had been this far. Wakhita told them this small village was called Little Stone Village or *Iyan Cik'ala*.

Some of the homes were earth lodges. These were similar to the ones across the river, but these appeared taller. There were teepees as well. They did not go to this village. They followed a path that led upward and away from this village. They reached a high point where one could see all around, and below them hidden in a small valley was a small camp.

They could see more trails leading away from the main one that they were following. They had reached this point where they could see beyond to the village where their teepee stood. Smoke was flowing in streams from the teepee tops. Kikto sat in awe as he took in the sight of all this. They could hear dogs barking, birds chirping, and children laughing, when it quieted down they can hear the river flowing. It was beautiful! He had seen a great deal in one day.

Kikto now asked Wakhita if one could spend the night up here. Wakhita gave him an odd look and said, "Only the holy men spent nights up here." A short distance from where they now stood was a meadow with a small campsite. It was a permanent structure. The holy men lived up there, taking turns watching the night sky and the stars, and painted events of the night sky on buffalo hides.

Wakhita told them there was a time before he was born when some of the stars fell to the earth along the slopes where they had just been. The people were afraid to go near the fallen stars. The holy men were the only ones who went and prayed that no more stars would fall in this area.

Kikto asked again if there was a place where he could spend the night without disturbing the holy men. Wakhita told him that there would be some young men called runners who would be able to answer that question. They were walking on when one of the runners appeared in the path before them. He told Wakhita that he was sent down to one of the camps to get a singer. Wakhita told him about Kikto's wanting to spend the night up on the hillside. He asked them to wait there as he would go ask the holy man who was at the camp.

The runner asked Kikto's name and then walked away from them along one of the smaller paths off the main path. Kikto now asked Wakhita why there were runners along this path. It was to deliver messages to and from this camp.

Wakhita continued: "Long ago when the stars fell from the sky, there was only one holy man on the hill, and he was unable to send anyone down to warn the people." Since then he said, they had two holy men, sometimes more, and at least four runners on top of this ridge. They would carry messages to and from camp. These runners also learned about the stars, as someday they would be the holy men on the hilltop.

Wakhita told them about how long ago a star crossed the night sky, pulling a flame. Then he told them about how the ghost dancers danced across the northern sky. At such times a song was sung for the night relatives. As Wakhita told him this story, Kikto remembered the song he sang. He thought he would like to sing it to the holy men. *Yes, he decided, that's what I will do: sing it for them since it has been singing in my heart many times.*

Soon the runner returned. He told Kikto that the holy man had given permission for Kikto to stay on the hilltop overnight. He was to spend the night near the circle of rocks where a holy man now stood. Kikto was invited to help bring the holy man down from the circle.

They arrived at the spot where the holy men camped. A man sat near the fire pit. He stood as the four young men approached. He shook hands with Kikto and Iyeshni knowing that they were strangers and lastly shook Wakhita's hand.

He asked for Kikto, approaching the right person. He dressed a little different and was not quite as dark and the other from the prairies. He said asked Kikto to which of the mountain people he belongs. Kikto told him of his village near the circle of rocks. The man speaking to him knew then that Kikto was not an ordinary person, but perhaps the one who was to do the long awaited turn of the century ceremony.

Kikto looked around and saw that a buffalo hide was hung in preparation for painting. A young runner took one of the cedar bags hanging not far from the buffalo hide. He lit the branch and took it all around the entire area. Kikto breathed deeply and exhaled slowly and then did this a second time and a third.

As he sat down, the song played in his heart. He began singing. The first young runner grabbed a set of gourds and began to shake them. As they rattled, he held his hands still, but the rocks inside kept rattling as if on their own accord. Kikto finished the song. It was quiet for some moments. The other runner threw some buffalo robes over the sweat bath or *inithi*. He then took a bladder bag filled with water.

Kikto and Iyeshni stayed while Wakhita left. He had to tend to his boat and other things. They thanked him for bringing them up and asked him to return in the morning to continue their tour.

Soon more voices could be heard. An elderly man carrying his pipebag or *wachantognaka* came into view, followed by a runner with some of his belongings. Soon, they heard the voices of women as they too came into view.

The camp bustled with activity. The first runner came to Kikto and Iyeshni, informing them that it was time to escort the holy man from atop the hill. They were invited to go along.

When they reached the top of the hill, the Holy Man was finishing his prayers at the circle of rocks. When it was time to come down, they prayed. The other runner now took some burning cedar boughs and walked around the circle. The holy man came to the entrance of the circle, and everyone followed him back down the hill.

Glowing hot rocks sat in the center of the inithi, and buffalo robes covered the outsides of the lodge. At the top they left a round hole for the steam to exit. The men now entered, beginning with the holy man who had come down from the sacred circle.

The holy man sat down and told the others of nightly events for the past moon. Everyone sat quiet, listening. Then songs were sung. The women outside the lodge sang along. Kikto felt the song's power, its beauty, its connection to the entire universe at that moment. The song was about the invisible things of life.

The holy man began talking again. Kikto listened intently. This was different, not like the storytelling he loved so much; this was about the invisible becoming visible, about the constellations in the four corners of the universe, about events that occurred at the edge of the universe. He prayed for understanding.

The holy man now sang a song. Then Kikto was asked to sing the song he had sung earlier. He sang the song from his heart again. It flowed, its tune carried by the wind to the four corners of the universe. Someday this song would return to the people.

At last it was time to take the next holy man up to the circle of rocks. He had invited Kikto to spend the night with him up on the hill, like other night guests before. Kikto now carried his robes and offered to help carry other items. Iyeshni also helped. They reached the top, and the runner who had been the helper before now burned cedar again, all around the circle.

The holy man prayed and sang a song. The stars shone brightly as he sang; some even seemed to dance! It was a bright, clear night. Kikto gazed at the stars, seeing patterns he had not seen before until the holy man pointed them out. The sky was different here on the Plains. He could stand on the mountain and recognize the stars aligned in the sky all the way to the eastern horizon. In his young life he was taken to the mountain at different times to learn where each star position would be.

The holy man now explained to the group the sacredness of creation, and its sacredness spanned everything from ordinary things to the most sacred. Kikto watched as this was gestured to Iyeshni and wondered how much of life he understood. It was obvious that he was observant of everything, sometimes bringing to Kikto's attention something that he had not noticed. It was his nature.

The holy man who was standing at the center sprinkled cedar berries mixed with chokecherry and other leaves over the small fire pit at the center, which was constantly burning. Kikto listened as the holy man began to sing a song that seemed to make the dancing stars twinkle brighter. Each sparkle seemed to have rhythm. Finishing the song the holy man sent his voice to the universe, saying, "Long after I leave this physical world, this song will reach you, just as the voices of my ancestors reach you tonight." And began singing again. At that moment a star flew across the eastern horizon in a northerly direction. The holy man now faced another direction, sending his voice.

Kikto gazed at the night sky in all directions, recognizing some of the patterns which were now far to the west. He noticed the group of stars that remained together as if they were inside a teepee. On the outer side of the teepee were three additional stars, and each had a name. Kikto knew the names. It was this group of stars that were viewed as bonding or uniting the three sacred fires called Ochethi Yamni. It was this group of stars that had been watched annually for thousands of years. The ceremony soon to be held connected to this group of stars.

It was now dawn, and the holy man sang the sunrise song, after which he retired to a shelter connected to the circle. A runner arrived and told Kikto that a storm was coming. Earlier another storm had passed by. But now there was another coming. Kikto looked up at the now sunlit sky. There were no visible clouds. But he believed that there was a storm coming.

They left the small camp. They ran, not sure when the storm would arrive. Kikto had looked to the west for the clouds, but soon dark clouds came in from the east. Wakhita had joined them on his way in just as they got to the main trail. Now they ran all the way down to the teepee camp.

When they arrived, the camp was bustling with excitement. A storm was coming and the whole camp prepared themselves for it.

It was now autumn or *ptanyetu*. The leaves had fallen off the trees, and most were bare. The teepees in the camp looked brighter and bigger once the leaves were gone, he noticed. They quickly prepared their teepee for protection and also secured a dog shelter. Sometimes the dogs just disappeared in such storms. Other times they relied on the owner for protection.

In the days that followed Kikto and Iyeshni helped carry heavier wood from afar.   Other men and young warriors would also help carry the wood closer to the village. Little boys carrying sticks were complimented on their strength. The wood was for the entire camp.

Autumn had turned to winter. It was now the second moon of winter. The next three moons would be extremely cold. The names of the winter moons were the only ones that the men and women shared. When the last winter moon waned and a certain star appeared, once again the men and women would go back to using their separate moon names for the next three seasons.

Winter passed; storms blew in and out. Waziya, they called the keeper of winter moons was an old wizard who lived in the north. He was the oldest of the first four brothers. He has no compassion, he has no pity for the two-legged or the four-legged or the winged ones. He was known to be a selfish wizard who used his time to amuse himself. Children were warned in the early fall not to say his name too loudly lest they should awaken him. When he heard his name, even a whisper, he would come flying after the one who called him! That was Waziya.

Spring arrived and with it the eyapaha announced a new beginning with a song. Many people gathered around to sing with him. The women would now be watching for the appearance of the guiding star to plant their crops.

Into early spring the ice began to melt, huge chunks of icebergs floated down the river, crashing and cracking and making a lot of noise. Soon great shoals of fish would be swimming down the river. Some of the men had their spears ready for fishing. The catch would be smoked and prepared for trading soon. For Kikto it was like the buffalo run in the spring, when herds of buffalo ran to the north. These fish were swimming downriver! It was told that these fish swam all the way to the big water or *mini wanca*.

Kikto and Iyeshni were invited to go back up to the small camp along the hill. They were going there to renew their bodies, heart, mind and spirit or *nagxi*. A new year had begun, and it was time to do such things.

When they arrived at the camp, they found a holy man painting a wolf hide showing the positions of the stars. It was to be sent to Xe Ska in the next few days. Kikto studied the map and noticed the picture of the sun coming over the horizon. Then a blue star was drawn above its path, but it was a day painting. Kikto thought deeply about this. He came to realize that the stars did not go away during the day, that a star traveled before the sun only to reappear in the western sky in the evening.

The next scene was of the night sky, a picture of the moon followed by a set of constellations also in its path. Kikto thought about that. He wondered when the painting was brought to the mountain, where the moon would be and the constellations. Could it be that the night sky would look like that in one moon from now?

The holy man was just finishing painting when they arrived. The runners burnt cedar boughs all around camp, covered the inithi, and prepared the water. The singer for the holy man was the only one who should carry the rocks to the center, using elk antlers to carry them. The holy man at the top had been brought down to purify and rest for the day. Kikto was ready for this purification.

He had told Iyeshni about leaving this village to continue on his journey to get the sacred red rock to bring to the mountain. Along with it he was to get the sacred yellow and blue earth from this area. It would be prepared for him upon their return. Now it was time to purify and to begin the journey eastward to get the sacred red rock.

Kikto told the holy men of the next step in his journey while they were in the inithi. That night he was to stand up on the hill. He must study the path of the stars and their position. He must be sure of the number and where the Ochethi Yamni Teepeela would appear in the sky. He must paint what he saw tonight and send it along with the other painted hide. He was prepared to spend the night near the circle of sacred rocks.

He watched the night sky all that night.

Early the next morning, following morning rituals, he went down to the small camp and began painting. He painted the Ochethi Yamni Teepeela in the eastern horizon. It was the spring of the year, and that was where the constellation appeared at dawn, just before sunrise, and that was what the picture depicted. At the end of the day, the two hides were wrapped and given to two runners who would take them to a village; other runners would take them from there until they reached the mountain where the circle of rocks stood.

Two more runners were dispatched to get the sacred blue earth from an area to the east of them. The yellow earth was found in this area. Kikto and Iyeshni left to continue on their journey to get the sacred red stone. They were now about two days away from where the sacred red stone could be found.

They camped with a small hunting group. They each carried only their water bags. Their pack dogs and herd of deer were left at this camp. They would be safe. Kikto's grandfather had told him that there would be two white rocks protruding high above the earth. They were to seek a small grove of trees near this place. Now in their path stood such a place. It was from here that he must run. He must be exhausted when he arrived in the early dawn to get the rock. Was it not what the buffalo had done? It was the proper way to get the rock. Kikto told Iyeshni he (Kikto) must run, that he(Iyeshni) was free to walk when he tired, but that Kikto had the responsibility of running. Iyeshni told him he too would run. So it was. They ran.

After having run all through the night and into dawn they arrived at the one of the holiest sites upon their land. A man was singing the sunrise song as runners arrived from different directions. The song ended, and all were now standing in a circle around the area where the stone would be gotten.

A man now spoke, saying that he had been there since he was a young boy; he was born farther to the north of this place. He told that his family moved here when his grandfather was chosen to be one of the caretakers of this sacred site. He told how his grandfather passed his duty on to him and how he in turn would pass it on to one of his grandsons. He said that the prayers and songs were to be kept as they were heard this morning. It was a daily ritual, to take care of this sacred site.

Now each of the young men who had arrived was asked to take a cedar bough, light it in the fire, and follow the lead singer as they circled the area of the rock. The area was deep, surrounded by a worn path that was used to purify the area several times a day. The caretakers were relentless; they took their responsibility seriously.

Now as the singer sang a song, the young men sang along with him. They continued singing until far into midmorning. These sacred songs must be sung before they took the stones that each traveled from afar to take. Each traveler must go to the center one at a time and tell where they came from, who had sent them, and what they would do with the stone.

The first two young men cried as they each spoke of the sick relatives in their home villages saying they needed the stones to help with the healing of loved ones, and then it was Kikto's turn. He reached the center, cleared the lump in his throat, and said, as he put his hands on the chosen stone, "You are chosen to go to Xe Ska where the holy men will use you for renewing the cycle of the way of life for the people. You are chosen to be the heart of Ochethi Yamni for the next

Kiktopawingxe." With tears streaming, Kikto continued, "For the next generations of the two-legged, of the four-legged to come, for all of the creatures of the earth, those with wings, those in the water, and those who crawl, you are chosen to help make life new. You are chosen to help when the new grass appears."

Kikto was weeping as he finished. He had not realized the intensity of his purpose. He also realized that he was praying for his grandchildren and his great grandchildren. He was praying for the future of a nation, a nation called Ochethi Yamni.

He thought of the red stone that would be used in the spring for the ceremony. He thought of his mother's bloodline who would be keepers of this stone he now put his hands on. He thought of a distant time when a future grandson would be here at the same place doing what he was now doing, doing what his grandfather has done in the past.

After Kikto finished, other young men followed. After all of them had finished, they stood in a circle. The keeper of the stone sang a song that told the story of how the buffalo gave them this stone.

Kikto thought of the story his grandfather told of how a giant buffalo stood in the north, and each generation he lost some of the hair off his legs. At this time there was no hair on one of his legs, and they were now at the second leg with some of the hair gone. He wondered how much they lost for each generation and how much will be lost in the future generations.

It was time for them to rest. They were fed broth and taken to teepees. They were told to rest, as in the evening there would be some storytelling. It did not take Kikto and Iyeshni long to fall asleep. Iyeshni awakened before Kikto and went to explore the area, not sure of where he could or could not go. There was a small lake near the place. Others were there. The young women who went there to get water were laughing and having a good time splashing each other. The young men waited for them to draw their water.

By now Kikto had gotten up and walked down to the water as well. Iyeshni was standing with some young men who were talking to him. Kikto arrived, and it became quiet. The young women now filled their bladder bags and were leaving. As they walked past, the young men tried not to look. However, it was natural to do so, and they were curious.

The young women were beautiful, Kikto noticed. They were not as tall as the mountain women, and they were darker. Iyeshni also noticed that the women were darker than the ones from his camp. The young women and their chaperones were now away from the lake. The young men jumped into the water to refresh themselves.

They returned to camp. Many people were now gathering at the center of the camp for storytelling. Kikto, who always loved this, was now ready to listen. The storytellers were older men; they knew the stars, and they spoke of the sacred events in the night sky. They spoke of the Turn of the Century ceremony. These stories, they said, would be retold up on the Xe Ska.

The next morning, the sacred stones were packed and ready for the journey in the various directions. A group of people were to travel with Kikto and Iyeshni. Kikto had told the eyapaha in the village of his journey back to the mountains. He would not delay anywhere. He was going to head straight back to the mountains. The sacred stone was expected by the end of the summer, so as to prepare it for the new year, the time when the ceremony would be held.

At the time of departure, the intentions of Kikto were announced. Some of the runners who had arrived from other directions told of how their camps were awaiting this ceremony and that some members of their camps had already traveled toward the mountains. Kikto wondered how many people were up on the mountain by now. He was patient; he would soon find out.

He and Iyeshni left the area with the sacred red stone wrapped in a white buffalo hide made especially for this trip. They arrived back at the camp where they had left their belongings and Kikto's herd. There the people who waited joined with the group now traveling with Kikto and Iyeshni.

They returned to Iyan Otxunwahe and went to the sacred circle of rocks. The holy men there said they would travel later to join the group with Kikto and Iyeshni. Kikto traded another young antelope for some of the chanhanpi that his grandmother wanted, in case he could not go to get his supplies from the previous summer.

Kikto and Iyeshni left from Iyan Otxunwahe with two of the runners, the one who went to get the sacred blue earth and the one who prepared the sacred yellow earth. Now there were only four travelers, and they would travel swiftly. So, they traveled without delay. The runners knew a way to travel faster to Xe Sapa and arrived in a few days.

The travelers continued their journey to Xe Ska. It took them two moons from the time they left Iyan Otxunwahe to get to the foothills of Xe Ska. The lead antelope was excited as they arrived at the foothills and led his herd up into the mountains. Kikto knew that they would meet in the mountain village.

Everywhere along the foothills it seemed there were teepee camps. Kikto could not recall ever seeing so many people, not even in the trade town. They did not travel near the camps because of the sacred stone and earth they were carrying. They traveled away from most of the villages.

They arrived at the village late one afternoon. It was now cooler in the mountains. Back at camp people were excited. Kikto had left his fellow travelers and their belongings in a chosen spot. He went to the camp to see his grandparents and parents. It was obvious that they were expecting him, as a great number came to greet him. As his grandfather came and shook his hand, his mother and grandmother were crying. His younger sister just kept smiling at him. Now he had to announce his fellow travelers, and together they must continue on up to the mountain with the sacred stone and earth.

His grandfather and some others joined them. They arrived at the top of the mountain where the holy men awaited Kikto's return. The paintings they had sent were spread out before them, including the one Kikto painted. His grandfather recognized Kikto's painting immediately. He wondered how his grandfather knew. The holy men were pleased with the stone and the sacred earth. It was time to begin the preparations for the ceremony.

It was now time to prepare for the coming of spring and the ceremony. The appearance of the first blade of green grass there on the mountain would be the sign that a new year had arrived. Many people had traveled to be up in the mountains for the winter so that they will take part in the long awaited ceremony.

Kikto, Iyeshni, and the two runners had traveled up and down the mountain to help those who wanted to camp up closer to the circle of rocks. As people made their teepee camps, they also prepared for winter. Kikto could not wait for storytelling at these camps. From these camps they could not see the circle of rocks as it was considered a sacred place.

It seemed to Kikto that the storytelling were different from what he had heard throughout his travels. These stories were about how others came to make camp up here in these mountians long ago, stories that were told specifically here, because stories were like that. One had to be at a certain place and time in order to tell particular stories. Kikto thought of this often.

Winter had ended some time back; the nights were still cold, yet the snow and ice were melting. The teepee camps were growing. Each day there were new arrivals as the time got closer.

It was Kikto's duty be on the mountain from the time of his return until the ceremony takes place. Iyeshni and the two runners stayed as well. They gazed at the night sky together, sometimes singing, sometimes just talking. They noticed the position of the group of stars called Ochethi Yamni Teepeela.

People were gathered all around the Inyan Kahomni. The night sky was clear, and the stars were bright. It was a very good night for the ceremony. Kikto's family was gathered behind them somewhere. The singing would start soon. The fire pit at the center was lit; other fire pits were made along the outer side of the circle of rocks. It was time.

Kikto and Iyeshni spent the day preparing for the ceremony. In addition to the two runners who had come with them, there were two more. Now they all stood around Kikto, who was given the medicine bundle that had been kept by his mother. His grandfather and grandmother were sitting nearby. He pulled out four rattles, one for each of the four young men. He gave one of the runners a drum to sing the songs.

Kikto instructed each young men in what they should do. The holy men who were at the top of the mountain now stood nearby, watching to make sure that Kikto gave the right instructions. Each young man had a duty to fulfill.

Kikto knew his work. He told the four young runners that at the end of the people's singing they were to stand behind each of the four holy men, who would be in each of the outer circles. Singers that the Holy Men had chosen would stand in the places of the young men, who would be following the holy men to the center.

Iyeshni was to take two of the rattles and shake them when the time arrived. They would let him know when to begin. When the time came, all of them should be prepared. The fire keepers from each of the three Council Fires would also be there with their sacred fires.

People were now gathered around; the participants in the center were painted. A song was sung for the people. Kikto sang the song that came to him, and the other young men sang with him. They sang several songs together with the people. It was now close to dawn. The night sky was turning lighter. Soon Ochethi Yamni Teepeela would arrive.

In time the first star appeared. Many people cheered, because they believed that it was what the ancestors had done. The gathering quickly quieted down again.

Now more of stars appeared. One of the holy men asked Kikto to name the three stars that followed Ochethi Yamni Teepeela. "The first," he said, "the one nearest to the southern horizon, is called Hetula, and he has a song. The second star is called Hehuta, and he has a song, the third is called Hebuwe, and he has a song." He was asked then if there were any more. Kikto answered, "There is one, but his name and his song must not be named or sung until he arrives."

"Hau, Hau" came the reply from the holy men.

A holy man then readied his voice and began the song for Hetula, the first star in Ochethi Yamni Teepeela. He sang the first verse, and the young man to the south sang it a second time, the young man to the west a third time, the young man to the north a fourth time, and then things passed back to the center. They sang another song in the same manner for Hehuta and then for Hebuwe. Then it became quiet. Expectancy filled the gathering as they waited for the return of the sacred star.

The holy man at the center held the stone up toward the sky, saying, "You are chosen for renewing the cycle of the way of life for the people. You are chosen to be the heart of Ochethi Yamni for the next Kiktopawingxe." With tears streaming down, he continued, "For the next generations of the two-legged, of the four-legged to come, for all the creatures of the earth, those with wings, those in the water, and those who crawl, you are chosen to help make life new." He finished.

At this point a new star appeared, joining the other three stars. Kikto began singing a song: *"Hekula, Hekula anpo luta ki le Wakxan yelo, Hekula, Hekula shina txo in yaku welo, Hekula, Hekula wichozani yuha yaku welo, Hekula, Hekula shina ska in yaku welo."* As Wichaxpi Luta arrived.

The beautiful song that his mother sang to him, so long ago, he now finished singing. Somewhere off in the distance, a bull elk bellowed. It echoed throughout the mountains. It was a sacred day.

Glossary

The Lakxota words used in the story of Kikto.

Ehani	long time ago, long ago
Cha	relative clause, connects two phrases
Teepee	home to the Lakxota
Watxoye	Makes Blue
Khugyuha Mani	Century Keeper
Wichaxpi	Star
Kiktopawingxe	Century Turner (1,000 yrs)
Unci	grandmother
Até	father
Eyapaha	Town Crier
Chinshka	horn spoon, Big Dipper/Ursa Major
Txakozha	grandchild
Ochethi Yamni	Three Council Fires
Kikto	the main character
Wichaxpi Luta	Sacred Red Star
Xe Sapa	Black Hills
Xe Ska	Rocky Mountains
Waniyanpi	pet
Oyate	people or nation
Thiyoshpaye	Extended Family
Wasna	berries/dried-meat/buffalo fat mixture
Okhizhata	a fork in a river where the tributaries flow into a main body of water

Kxoshkalaka	young men (unmarried)
Wikxoshkalaka	young women (unmarried)
Omakiya	help me
Wiwila	spring
Shungmanitu	wolves
Yashlé	coyote
Ikto	Lakxota Trickster
Thiblo	older brother of a female
Thiyokthi	a willow hut, temporary shelter
Hosapa	catfish
Shungmanitu Txanka	Timber Wolf
Chegnake	breech cloth
Matxo Paha	Devil's Tower (old Lakxota name)
Matxo Paha	Bear Butte (borrowed from the Northern Cheyenne)
Iyeshni	Does Not Speak
Chokata	the center of the village
Lechel oyake (phrase)	he/she told it like this
Makhicima	a lean animal
Ikpazo Wachipi	to dance in their finest regalia, grand entry
Ikpazopi	similar to a parade, grand entry
Ohunkankan	night time storytelling
Mashké	female friends or sister-friend
Kxola	male friends or brother-friend
Tinpsila	wild turnips
Kikta po!	Wake Up! Said by the Eyapaha
Anpa yelo	It is daylight! Said by the Eyapaha
Akish'a	men's victory cry
Mitakuye pi	my relatives
Anagxoptan po	Listen!
Ki le	connects two phrases
Le	this
Etanhan	to be from a place or band
Hecha	to be that
Inyan Kahomnixepxa	circle of stones at a point or ridge
Unshikela	to be pitiable

Ikxopxab	to be afraid of… or to be leery of someone or something
Shni	not
Yo	men use this at the end of some sentences, polite command
Taku-iyuha	all things, everything
Washté	good
Chekpa Teepeela	Twin Dwellings
Chanku	path, trail or road
Wakpala	creek
Mnihanska	river
Shayeni Ozhu	Cheyenne River
Mni Wanca	ocean
Cheyaktxun	bridge or crossing over a creek
Khiyuwegxa	a crossing in or through the water
Mashtinca	rabbit
Pxemnamnayapi	roasted meat
Echani	soon
Ki	the or topic marker
Hanta yo!	Get away! Polite command by a male speaker
Wanyeca	firefly
Txunkashila	grandfather
Mnishoshé	Missouri River
Watunwan	scout
Wichakichopi	invited guests
Tokxala	fox
Chincala	young animal
Igxugxa	den
Kxate	wind
Wanyanka yo!	Observe! By a male speaker
Macik'ala	I am small
Na	and
Hu	legs
Ma?ota	I have many
Eyash	but then

Chikte	I kill you
Owakihi	I can
Yelo	male speaker (intention)
Mataku	what am I?
Hwo	male interrogative
Paha	hill
Pestola	sharp or pointed
Makxoché	land, earth
Hochoka	sacred center
Iyan Otxunwahe	Stone Village or Town
Minixaxa Otxunwahe	Waterfalls Village or Town
Thitxunwan (Teton)	Prairie Dwellers (Lakxota)
Blo	potato
Wahanpi	soup
Pshin	onions
Channakpa	mushrooms
Mitakuye Owas'in	All my Relatives (ending of prayer)
Watxeca	leftover food
Wakinyan aku!	The Thunderbeings are returning!
Wasu	hail
Chaske	oldest born boy
Ishnala	Alone/Only One as he had not yet had younger sibling
Wasutxun Wi	Harvest Moon
Matxo Teepeela	Bear Dens
Kxantashasha	Moon of Ripen Plums
Wakxan	sacred or holy
Ipxa	the point on a ridge
Igmuglezela Iyuwegxa	Bobcat Crossing
Chanpxa Wakpa	Cherry Creek
Kxanta Wakpa	Plum Creek
Skuya	bitter (or sweet depending on how it is used)
Wanagxi Txachanku	Milky Way (Ghost Trail)
Makxatxa Oniya	humidity at its bluest

Iyan Txanka	boulders, big rocks
Thigmigma	earth lodge
Wata	bull boat or boat
Hoxwozhu	Plants Using Fish
Chanhanpi	maple sap (sugar)
Iyan Cik'ana	Little Stone Village
Wakhita	to search for something, looking for something